Bitter Honey

featuring

Nick Verriet P.I.
The Early Years

By

Nicolas D. Charles

Published by A.N. Charles Enterprises
P.O. Box 1187 Hayward, WI 54843

Cover design by Dee Lindner
Cover photographs courtesy of Alexandra Charles

9   8   7   6   5   4   3   2   1

ISBN: 978-0-692764-73-2

Printed in the United States of America

Always Dee

Chapter One

She walked into my Michigan Avenue office without knocking. Nine times out of ten, an unannounced visitor means trouble and one look confirmed my suspicion that this was no exception. She was drop-dead gorgeous, wearing a body hugging red knit dress with blue stripes that would have been horizontal on a lot of women, but not her. I felt seasick, my eyes following her waves as she sailed across the room toward my desk.

Gliding her prow into one of my office chairs, she said in a silky voice, smooth like warm honey, "Mr. Verriet, I need your help. Some men are after me."

"Perfectly understandable."

She shook her head. "What?"

"What men?"

"The ones after me."

"Why are they after you?"

"Well . . . I don't think they're after me, I think they're after this case," she replied, raising a tenor saxophone case, worn and weathered from a multitude of gigs across countless miles.

I hadn't paid any attention to the case until now because she held it by her side next to her leg, and there was a lot of leg I hadn't finished examining. She shifted easily in her chair, crossed her slender gams and pulled her dress down which was all right by me as the action exposed more of her bountiful cleavage.

"Are you just going to keep staring at me, or are you going to help me?"

"Help you? Uh, right! What about?"

"Didn't you hear me? Some men are trying to take this case from me. Joe left a piece of paper inside the case with your name and address. His note said you were a private investigator. I thought you could help me, but now I'm not so sure."

"Joe who?"

"Joe Marcus."

"Oh."

"Oh! Is that all you can say?" she asked in exasperation. "Will you help me or not?"

"That depends."

"Of course, I'll pay you," she added hurriedly.

I nodded.

Her hand shook as she reached in her purse, brought out some crumpled bills, and spilled them on my desk.

I looked at the bills and nodded some more.

When I didn't say anything, she became noticeably agitated. "I can get more if that's not enough."

"Miss, umm?"

"Oh, sorry, it's just that I've been so worried, afraid—these men and all."

"Uh-huh."

"I'm Gale Storm."

"You certainly are."

"What? You talk funny don't you?"

"You should see me dance."

"Huh?"

"Never mind. What else is in the case the men are after?"

"Only the note was in it."

"Nothing else?"

"Joe left the case with me and said it was very important to him. He said keep it and not tell anyone about it, and especially not to open it. He said—"

I cut her off, "So curiosity got the better of you. You opened it, and there was a piece of paper inside with my contact information written on it. Is that right?"

"Look, he disappeared two days ago and nobody's heard from him since. Wouldn't you have opened it?" she asked defiantly.

I ignored her challenge. "Doesn't it seem kind of silly putting yourself in harm's way for an empty saxophone case? Why not just give it to whoever wants it?"

"What kind of detective are you? Isn't that obvious? These men must think I took something that wasn't there. They won't

2

believe me if I tell them the truth. Look, all I know is that Joe gave this case to me Friday night and told me to hold it."

It took my brain a while to wrap itself around her cock-eyed explanation to find she had a point. "Do you still have the paper?"

She dived into her pocketbook again, and in a few seconds produced a small folded piece of paper that she straightened out. She leaned over my desk and laid the paper in front of me. I blindly reached for the note and held it up to the light. The only thing I saw was my name, office address, and occupation scrawled on it. I came around my desk, perched on the corner and looked down at her.

"Okay. So, tell me about the men."

Without her saying a word, I knew what the men looked like because, as if on cue, two nasty looking gazabos marched through my office door.

"Doesn't anyone knock anymore?"

The duo waved a pair of menacing snub-nosed .38s, first at me, then at Gale, and back at me. The two gorillas' bulk could make up four normal-sized guys. Wide and about five and a half feet tall, they packed a lot of muscle. So similar were their dress and physiques, they could be mistaken for twins until you looked at their faces.

One was bald with a big scar running from his left temple toward the back of his head. A triangular wedge of ear was missing where the scar line briefly stopped before resuming its path. His dark eyes darted around the room before they settled on the note and money lying on my desk.

His sidekick had dark close-cropped hair shaped into a widow's peak over his ponderous forehead. His mouth was smallish, puckered, as if he was sucking on a lemon. His beady, deep-set eyes stared at Gale. His overly red lips formed a sneer, accenting the small scars on his chin.

Menacing, these lads were war torn and tested. They wore identical broad pinstriped charcoal suits with outdated grey felt spats. The outfits may have retained a look of class on older gentlemen, but on these two gazabos the garb looked ridiculous. If not for their weaponry, I probably would have laughed aloud at their get-ups.

Casually easing back from my desk, I moved my hand until it rested on the pull of my top drawer where my gun resided.

The bald one barked, "Freeze, dick. Keep your hands where we can see 'em," with a voice that sounded like glass being shined with coarse-grain sandpaper.

"And if I don't?" I challenged.

"You're smarter than that," he declaimed.

Maybe they'd shoot and maybe they wouldn't, but I couldn't take the chance. Gale let out a whimper and stood to move away from him.

"You too, sister. Stay where you are and put the case down."

Gale carefully set the case on her abandoned chair. Sourpuss lurched around my desk and without a word swung his gun at me. I raised my arm to block the blow, but he anticipated my move, grabbed my arm with his left hand, and swiped his gun across my temple. My head exploded into a thousand tiny lights of pain. In vain, I weakly reached for my desk before crumpling to the floor. Through a darkly narrowing lens, I saw the two goons move in on Gale, her shrill scream fading away into silent shadows.

Chapter Two

Light at the tunnel's end grew larger as my senses slowly
returned. Pain seized my body in spasms. Waves of nausea
followed. When I tried to stand my rubbery legs folded under me.
I brushed something away from my left eye and reached for the
edge of my desk to pull myself up, but my hand slipped off
before I could secure my grasp. I lifted my hand to my eyes and
saw blood running down my wrist. I wiped it on my shirt and
tried to stand again, but my legs decided it was better to stay on
the floor.

After a few minutes, I managed to sit up and prop my right side
against my desk. I yanked open my bottom desk drawer, reached
for my bottle of Old Granddad, and drank until I had to gasp for
air. After two more swigs, the pain in my head became tolerable
and I laid gramps to rest.

Pulling myself up into my chair, I observed that my visitors
were gone and so was the gal with Joe's case. The cabbage she
had placed atop my desk lay splattered with blood. I swept the
bills into my top drawer before I tested my legs again. I could
walk, but the effort made my stomach turn cartwheels. I held
back the nausea until I reached the men's room where I gave up
the whiskey.

One look in the mirror told me I needed stitches. I grabbed a
handful of paper towels, soaked them in cold water, and dabbed
gingerly at the gash. Having temporarily staunched the blood
flow, I splashed water over my face and neck and cleaned up as
best I could. With a makeshift cold compress of more wet towels,
I returned to my office.

Rolling up the towels, I squashed them on my bloody pate, and
held them in place by my fedora. I donned my suit coat and
buttoned it to the top to hide as much of my bloodstained shirt as
possible. Returning to the men's room, I looked in the mirror at
the sad personage staring back at me. With disgust, I tore away
the blood soaked mess and replaced it with a new wad of paper.

When I reached the main floor of my office building, dizziness returned and I paused to draw in extra oxygen before proceeding next door.

At the adjacent building, I waited for a woman holding her kid's hand to exit the revolving door. She took one look at me, and quickly drew her daughter close to her side.

I mumbled, "Excuse me ma'am," and stumbled inside.

Shuffling unsteadily, I made my way across the slick marble tiles in the lobby to the bank of elevators. When I pressed the call button, a gent in a business suit suddenly decided against using the elevator. I should have used the stairs, too, as the ride made my head feel like a melon in a machine press. Clutching the side rail to steady myself, I was unceremoniously deposited on the fourth floor with a lurch. I stuck my foot out to prevent the doors closing while breathing laboriously to clear my head.

The doctor's receptionist, Sandy, took one look at me and said, "My god, Nick, what happened to you?"

"I was attacked by a mad troop leader when I passed on purchasing her girls' cookies."

"I doubt your pass concerned cookies," she said with a knowing look.

"Maybe I don't like cookies. Did you ever think of that?"

"That's a hot one—you passing on any woman's cookies," she countered with a glint in her eye.

"Look, Sandy, I appreciate the lively banter, but if I don't see the Doc soon, I'm going to bleed all over your reception area." I removed my hat and lifted the blood-soaked bandage, giving her a good look at my wound.

She nodded briskly, and told me to wait while she left in search of Doctor Bax.

Jim Bax was a trusted friend who had patched me up more times than I cared to remember. His nurse, a matronly woman named Maria, returned in a minute and told me to follow her. She waved me into an examination room and had me lay down on the treatment table while she deftly began to clean the gash.

6

"This is a deep cut, Nick. You need stitches," she said as she shaved the hair around the cut.

"I'd have done it myself, but I flunked home economics."

Maria was no nonsense. "Doc will be right in," she said, neatly laying out sutures and a needle on a nearby tray.

A few minutes later, Jim entered with a concerned look. He examined my head and grunted, "You're lucky, Nick. From the shape of the cut, I'd say it was a glancing blow and not a direct hit. Probably take a dozen stitches. Should I even ask?"

"Jim, you probably wouldn't believe me if I told you."

"Uh-huh. You take more hits than a baseball," he said as he turned on a small lamp, directing its bright light on my skull.

"Damn, Doc, do you have to use that beacon? My head hurts enough as it is."

"The light hurts because you have a minor concussion," he explained. "I'm not going to numb the area unless you insist. The injections would probably hurt worse than the stitches."

"Just don't whistle while you work."

After he finished, he went over to the sink, washed and dried his hands, and poured water into a glass that he proffered me with a dose of aspirin. "You should be good as new in a couple of days. Leave the stitches in for at least a week before you come back. Until then, lay off the booze and get lots of rest."

"I'll rest after I settle the score with the mugs who gave me this tattoo."

"It's your headache, Nick," he replied resignedly.

"Yeah, and I'm going to pass it along as soon as I can. Thanks, Jim."

He gave me a thoughtful look. "You're just itching for an early grave aren't you, Nick?"

"If I wanted a psychiatrist, I would have gotten off on the third floor," I growled.

"Alright. Have it your way, tough guy. But one of these times I'm not going to be able to fix you up and send you on your way."

"What am I supposed to do, Doc? Quit my trade and lead a boring life like you?"

"You just might have something there," he grinned. "If I had to do it over again, I'm not so sure I wouldn't trade places with you."

"Uh-uh, the world needs good doctors a helluva lot more than it needs private dicks like me. I'll be seeing you, Jim."

"Watch out for those girl scouts, Nick," Sandy said with a wink after I paid my bill.

The aspirin helped until I reached the street where the late June sunshine drilled excruciating pain into the back of my head. I headed to my apartment where I took a hot shower and rinsed off with cold water, keeping my noggin under the faucet until it felt numb.

Refreshed, I donned my duds and took a stroll toward Frankie's Bar, my favorite speakeasy haunt, en route stopping at the cleaners. When I passed my soiled clothes to the Chinese fellow behind the counter, he handed me a ticket, and announced, "Wednesday," as if laundering blood-splattered clothes was an everyday occurrence.

The dimly lit interior of Frankie's eased my headache and instantly picked up my spirits.

"Butters in?" I asked Frankie who was tending bar.

He nodded towards the back room.

Butters is the moniker for Charles Butterworth the Third. Most people believe his nickname is derived from his surname, but those closest to him knew he picked up the handle shortly after he came to realize he could make a living from his unique talent. He had the uncanny ability to remember everything he heard making him the best professional tipster in Chicago. Henceforth, he no longer freely dished out the dirt. You had to 'butter' him up with cold hard greenbacks if you wanted the latest lowdown on friend or foe. He kept a wire on everybody, and could provide you with almost any information you sought. His contacts ran the gamut through all walks of life. He was one of my best friends and I was one of his best clients.

Butters was engaged in his usual card game when I stuck my head through the doorway. He looked up and I gave him a nod. Seeing him always made me smile. His ears stuck out at a funny angle from his round head. The feature actually added something to his look—somehow made him a regular joe you felt comfortable around—someone you'd easily open up to and tell all.

I went to Butter's booth that Frankie kept reserved for his business at the rear of the joint. After a few minutes wait, Butters slid into the seat opposite me.

"What'll ya have, Butters?"

"My usual."

I waved to Frankie and motioned for a round. He brought a near beer for Butters and a double rye for me—the good stuff that Johnny Torrio and his gang hauled down from Canada.

"Nick, ya gotta stop drinkin' so much," Butters said wrinkling up his nose.

"Why is everybody giving me advice today?"

"Maybe it's because we care about ya. Ya ever think of that, ya big palooka?" he replied as his eyes moved to my stitched scalp.

"I'm here for some information, not a lecture," I snarled.

He put his hands up in defense, "Damn, Nick, you're touchy today. What's up?"

"You'd be touchy, too, if somebody started your day off by shaving your scalp with a .38."

"Yeah, I guess I would at dat," he commiserated. "Who did it?"

"That's what I hope you can tell me. But before we cover that ground, where is Joe Marcus' band playing?"

"Dey've been jivin' uptown at Roscoe's for da last couple o' months."

"Roscoe's? That's a new one. Who owns it?"

"Boots Handel. Remember him?"

"I thought he was in the slammer."

"He got sprung bout two months back. His mouthpiece pulled a slick one. He got another guy to confess to da charges so dey had to spring Boots loose."

"Probably some bum who agreed to a free ride at the taxpayers' expense and a big payday for his family," I said nodding sagely. "So how did Handel manage to open a nightclub uptown so soon after getting out of the pen?"

"He bought O'Malley's up on Rush Street. Word is he put da squeeze on da old man, but nobody knows how Handel raised da cabbage to buy da joint. Some say he had da do-re-mi stashed away before he went into da pen."

"Aw, shit. O'Malley sold out. I thought he only temporarily closed the place for some repairs."

"Yeah, ever since prohibition all da old-time saloon keepers are sellin' out to da mob boys. I hear Boots got da backin' of some mob toughs, too—Capone and his crew."

"Do you know who's on Boots' payroll?"

"Not da scrubbers, but I know da higher ups."

After Frankie brought another round, I described my two assailants. Butters nodded his head in acknowledgment.

"Dose is Boots' boys all right. The one with da scar and ear is Tom Corigliano. He's called Tom the Torpedo. The other bim is Sam da Barber. Boots brought 'em over from Detroit. Dey worked dere for Vinnie Vasco until he got bumped. Dem two always work together I hear."

"You think Boots had anything to do with Vasco's demise?"

"Maybe. Vasco was bumped off 'bout a week before Boots showed up in Chi. It'd explain him taking it on the lam from Detroit. I'll find out what I can from a guy I know dere."

"Good. Now what do you know about a real scorcher named Gale Storm?"

He let out a low whistle. "She's da canary at Boots' place. She parades her stuff two, three times a night."

"Is Boots her daddy?"

"Could be. Maybe dat's why she hasn't made time with any of da boys who've made a play for her, and dere's been plenty of 'em, believe me, brother. Word is she came over from Detroit, too. She started at Boots' place a couple weeks after he opened."

"Is Marcus around?"

"Nope. From what I hear, he took it on da lam a couple o' days ago."

"Do you know why he scrammed or where he went?"

"Nope, but Boots is lookin' for him—bad."

"Yeah, that fits with what Gale said."

"You testin' me, Nick?"

"No, just trying to figure all the angles. Get on the earie and find out what else you can about the singer and Marcus." I passed him a sawbuck and stood up.

"Sure, ting. Uh, watch it around Boots' boys, Nick. When der not makin' wit' da choppers, Sam da Barber likes to shave customers real close, usually from ear to ear."

I nodded in acknowledgment. "I'll remember that the next time he tries to lather me up."

Chapter Three

I stopped for a quick sandwich before I steered my rust bucket up Clark Street into Old Town. Joe Marcus and his wife lived in a small one-story brownstone set quietly amongst maple trees that lined the broad boulevard; a rusted ornamental fence surrounded their cozy abode. I squeaked open the front gate, walked up the cement steps and gave the doorbell a yank. Nobody answered. I gave the ringer another couple of pulls to no effect. As I turned to leave, the door swung open and Teresina Marcus greeted me, her hair wrapped in a towel, the rest of her bundled in a terrycloth robe.

"Nick, I was just thinking about you."

"The way you're dressed?"

She smiled broadly. "C'mon in. I was debating whether I should call you," she said and led me into the living room. Without asking, she went to the small bar tucked into the far corner and made us drinks. She sat down on the worn sofa close enough for me to breathe in her cleanliness.

"You want me to find Joe," I said matter-of-factly as she handed me my drink.

"How do you know?" she asked with a shocked look.

I tried to avoid sounding sarcastic. "It's my business, remember?"

"I've forgotten how you always seem to know what's going on. It's been a long time, Nick," she said with a dejected look. "Joe thinks you never stop by anymore because you still have an axe to grind for him kicking you out of the band."

"No," I answered shaking my head. "Joe should know better than that. We made our amends."

"Yeah, but he's never forgiven himself for his blunder. You know how he is. He treats everyone in the band as if he's their father. He told me he knew you had stopped using and was sorry he jumped to conclusions, but you know how many times he's been burned. Junk has robbed him of his best jazzmen."

"The past is past, Teri."

"Is it, Nick?" she asked with wide inquisitive eyes.

I gave her a hard look, leaned back, and replied tersely, "I didn't come here to talk about me, Teri. I came here to find out about Joe."

I didn't mean to sound so vehement, but she knew I always carried a torch for her and it made me feel vulnerable. She recoiled from my declaration as if I had slapped her. In a way, I had. A moment later, a small tear slid down her face as she studied me in silence. She reached over; her fingers cool as she touched my stitches. It took all my strength to sit still, to quell my racing emotions.

With a small nod, she said, "Joe's been gone almost three days. After practice on Friday, he called and told me something came up and he had to go away for a little while. He sounded tense and told me I should go to my mother's until he called me. When I asked him why, all he said was he needed time to work out a problem and he'd feel better if I was at my mother's. But you know how things have always been between me and mom—I'd rather weather things out here."

"Joe didn't say anything other than he had a problem?"

"That's all. I pressed him, but he said it was better that I wasn't involved. I'm worried, Nick. He hasn't called back," she despaired. "He must be in some kind of trouble."

"How long has he been playing at Roscoe's?"

"About two months."

"What's he say about the gig?"

While making us another round of drinks, she thought for a few seconds before answering. "The money is great. The owner agreed to a six-month stint for twice what Joe was pulling in at Ciprios. Joe was happy at first, but lately he's been troubled about something. When I ask him how it's going, he says it's copacetic and changes the subject."

"What about his singer?"

My question interrupted her thinking and a worried look came over her countenance. She stood up and poured more water in her glass even though she had barely touched her drink. For some reason, she felt it necessary to buy time. *Did I hit a sore spot?*

"The old one or the new one?" she asked in an agitated voice, pacing from the cellaret to the sofa and back again.

"Both," I replied.

"His old singer was Honey Farley."

"I remember her from right after the war. She was good."

Teri continued as if I wasn't there. "Joe thought the world of her, but she got a nose habit and Joe had to let her go. That's when the owner brought in Gale. Joe said she was all right. Personally, I think she's a gold digger, but I guess she sings okay."

"Anything else you can tell me about the club? What about Boots?"

"You know the owner, huh? I should have known."

"What about him?"

"Joe says Boots is a typical gangster, but he says if he doesn't work at the mob-owned joints, he'll be out of work. He pays on time and leaves Joe alone which makes him better than most."

She resumed her place on the sofa—close enough to make me uncomfortable. Casually her leg touched mine. I shifted my position to move slightly away.

"You said everything was okay until lately?" I pushed.

She bit her lower lip, looked down, and said, "Yeah, Joe hasn't been himself for the last few weeks. He's been distant, preoccupied with something, and when I ask him about what's bothering him he gets mad."

"No idea why?"

She shook her head without looking at me, which told me she did have an idea, but wasn't going to tell me. When she did look me in the eyes, she asked, "Nick, do you think Joe's in trouble with Boots?"

"Good question. I'll nose around; see what I can find out."

She forced a smile. "Joe sure misses you. He says you're the best arranger he's ever worked with. I've missed you too, Nick," she said softly and looked at me with her beautiful almond-shaped glimmers.

I gulped the rest of my drink and set my empty glass on a side table. "I better get going."

"Do you have to go so soon?"

"You want your husband back, don't you?"

There it was, laid bare between us and I felt small for having put it to her so bluntly. She didn't respond to my taunt, but when I stood, she grabbed my arm.

"Nick, I've been thinking a lot about how things were with us. I made a mistake marrying Joe. I know that now. Joe's good to me, but it's not the same, not like what we had. I should have waited for you," she said as she raised herself up on her toes, put her arms around my neck and kissed me gently.

I wanted to pull away. I should have pulled away. But as much as I hated to admit it, the old flame was still there. Her powdered scent was clean and wonderful and suddenly I was eighteen again, and in love with the most beautiful girl in the world—all before Uncle Sam enacted the Selective Service Act of 1917 and called me up for duty—before I returned home with a purple heart attached to a morphine habit.

I mashed my mouth against hers and kissed her back. She moaned when I pressed her trembling framework against me. I didn't want to let her go, but something triggered inside me and I pushed back and held her at arm's length.

"What's wrong?" she asked breathlessly.

"We can talk about us later, Teri. I better start looking for Joe." I left without looking back when she called my name.

Chapter Four

I drove away from the Marcus' all balled up inside. The yearning I felt made my chest tight and my breathing difficult. Then I began to get mad. All the old feelings surfaced with a boiling rage. As quickly as my anger had arisen, it subsided with the rationalization I was only human. *What guy doesn't have a weak spot for that one special woman in his life?*

I needed some time to think—and maybe to forget. Halfway to town, I stopped at The Oasis and took a seat down at the end of the bar, away from the regulars who sat huddled together listening to the Cubs' game being broadcast on the radio behind the bar. The bartender gave me a scowl and took his time to walk over and take my order. When he served up my near beer, I gave him a smile and a dime tip. Neither gesture changed his stony countenance.

I sat, nursed my beer, and thought back to the time when we were kids in the old neighborhood. The three of us had been inseparable then. Right from the start, Teri and I became close and Joe was our best friend. It all started when old man McElroy took it upon himself to get us kids interested in music and away from our more nefarious pastimes.

Our trio joined the neighborhood band with Joe on licorice stick, me on guitar, and Teri as our singer. Even though Sam was a colored, he was our bandleader, and a truly gifted talent. We all grew up on the South Side, me in an orphanage after my parents died in an accident. The band became Sam's South Siders, and after we started to earn money by making music, all the members fully turned the corner from a life of disreputable dealings.

Over time, players came and went. Teri quickly learned her dusky looks and figure prevailed over her voice. She quit the band when she discovered she could make a lot more money modeling for advertising. She always loved to sing, though, and occasionally did pick-up gigs. Joe and I continued playing with the band as Sam established a name for himself.

Joe studied Sam's every move and set himself up to break away with his own group so he could haul in bigger money playing in venues that didn't cater to coloreds. Meanwhile, I took advantage of Sam's right hand, an older guy named Foster, and learned everything I could from him about arranging music.

But as much as I loved music, the thrill of being a private detective took root in my soul from the time I had begun to read the exploits of Nick Carter, and all the sleuths subsequently in *Detective Story Magazine*. With my meager earnings from the band, I purchased every magazine I could lay my hands on. When I learned my parents had established a trust fund for me, I used my newfound wealth to finance formal music classes, offset by private investigator studies through Pinkerton's. Eventually, I figured something would tilt the scales one way or the other. Until then, life was the berries. Me, Teri, and my best friend, Joe.

The three of us went out for a big celebration the day I obtained my P.I. license and I landed a job with one of the national agencies. Teri moved in with me and we made plans for our future. The world was my oyster.

Then, I was drafted and came home a year later on a stretcher, all my childhood illusions shattered. A chasm of despair remained where my ideals once soared. Teri visited me at the hospital every day for the first month, but as time wore on her visits became less regular and eventually stopped altogether. After nine months, the doctors released me and I discovered my girl had married my best friend. I didn't blame either of them. I was happy for them. Like hell I was.

Afterward, I opened my own detective agency and began to piece my life back together. Joe insisted I join his band and score arrangements to earn extra cash until my agency got on its feet. I accepted his offer because I foolishly believed everything would work out for the best even though I knew deep down the only reason Joe kept me on his payroll was due to his guilt over marrying Teri.

The demand for jazz band arrangements heated up and I received invitations to join prestigious groups—groups that were achieving national notoriety. Jazz clubs were springing up all over town. Except for the real dives, every speak featured live music. Joe knew about the invites, but I stuck with him as if nothing was happening. I wasn't ready to cut loose and Joe couldn't bring himself to sever ties, either.

We both should have known better. A year later Joe and I had our inevitable falling out, triggered when he discovered a bag of heroin wedged next to the soundboard in the piano. He jumped to the easy conclusion that it was mine. The truth eventually surfaced—one of the band members had stashed his supply in the piano to avoid Joe's inspection.

Joe and I eventually made our peace, but things were never the same between us. I didn't rejoin his band, but occasionally I worked out arrangements for him when he asked. The work provided me a purpose and a little extra spending money, especially when I wasn't working on a case. Music also helped occupy my mind when that old craving surfaced. After four years, the desire was less, but it remained lurking in the shadows, waiting to rear its unforgiving head at the slightest weakness. Like now.

The sun melted beneath the skyscrapers as I wheeled my flivver downtown. I took Wacker Drive to LaSalle, crossed the river and parked a block down from Roscoe's. The façade was getting a new face-lift and inside Boots had added more bar room. Malone's former Irish décor now sported art deco embellishments. I had to hand it to Boots. The place was stylish with a touch of elegance, the real cat's meow.

I had a drink to take the edge off while the band finished practicing. I recognized a few old faces and they nodded in acknowledgement as I steered my chassis over to the bandstand. Bobby Mills, a great trombone player, appeared to be leading the band. He gathered up the players' sheets and looked up as I approached.

"Nick, man am I glad to see you. Maybe you can help me work out the kinks in a couple of the numbers," he suggested hopefully and offered me his hand while his eyes took in my stitch work.

"Sure, Bobby. You filling in for Joe?"

"Yeah. He ghosted sudden like."

"Mind if I ask you and the boys some questions? His missus is worried. I told her I'd look into his whereabouts."

"Yeah, sure," he replied and led the way to a table at the back.

Once we were seated, I asked, "Do you know why Joe left or where he might be?"

Bobby looked down; shook his big head. "No, to both questions. Everything was copasetic until Saturday when Joe didn't show. Here it is Monday and still no word from him."

"Did he seem nervous or different in any way before he disappeared?"

"Well . . . now that you mention it, Nick, he hasn't been himself lately, and he was real edgy Friday after we came back from break. He started to ride a couple of the boys about their playing—said they were slacking off. Then he went through the motions during our last set, like he wasn't all here. His solos were the sorriest."

"What about Gale, new singer? Joe have anything going on the side with her?"

"If he has, it's news to me. Sure, she dolls up to him, but he takes it in stride. I think she puts on the hotsy-totsy for job security, and Joe knows it."

"What about Boots? How's working for him?"

"Okay. He leaves us alone and pays on time. What more can you ask?"

"How about Joe? Did he and Boots get along? Did they ever argue about anything?"

"Naw, everything was jake as far as I know, Nick. Joe wasn't crazy about Boots bringing the new singer on board at first, but she turned out to be alright, and we did need a new torch after Joe fired Honey."

"Do you think any of the boys know anything that might help me?"

He shrugged and nodded toward the rear door. "Ask 'em. They're out back. Meantime, I'll get those numbers and we can go over 'em when you're done. Okay?"

"Yeah, sure. I'll only be a few minutes," I replied.

The back door behind the stage was ajar. The band members were standing on the small landing smoking reefers.

"How are the arrangements working?" I asked no one in particular.

"Chillin', Nick. You come for the show?" Jackie Shaw asked, offering me a drag on the joint he held. He eyed my shaved scalp as I took a drag to be sociable and handed it back to him. He was one of the original band members from way back. He was hell on the ivories. He reminded me of a tall skinny version of Fats Waller. He played like Fats, too, in that Harlem stride style.

"I'm trying to locate Joe," I announced. "Thought I'd see if any of you knew where he's gone or why he went."

A number of heads shook in negation to my query. One of the band members turned away when I looked at him. He was about five-ten with a slight build. He sported long wavy black hair and a small goatee that adorned a boyishly handsome face. He appeared nervous, his fingers constantly waggling by his side. I sidled over to him and introduced myself.

"Hi, I'm Nick Verriet. I do the arranging for Joe. You must be new to the band. How do you like the numbers?"

He had trouble focusing. He squinted at me through bloodshot blue eyes. He took another drag on the joint he held between yellow-stained fingers, murmured, "They're okay," and ignored my outstretched hand.

"What do you play?"

"Tenor," he replied off-handedly.

"What happened to Jerry?" Jerry was his predecessor—a smokin' tenor sax player.

"Man, what's with all the questions? You an arranger or a bull?" he asked in a rising, tense voice.

"Just a friend trying to help a friend, friend," I replied calmly. "You know anything about Joe's disappearance that might help me find him?"

He shook his head, turned his back to me, and went back to working on his reefer. There was something not right about him. He was too edgy.

"If anything comes to mind you think might help me locate Joe, give the word to Bobby. He'll know where to reach me," I said to no one in particular and walked away.

Bobby and I bandied ideas back and forth for an hour over one of the numbers until we were both happy with the results. He handed me a couple other tunes for me to work on at my leisure. Before he left to get ready for the first show, he asked, "You wouldn't consider playing with the band? We miss that extra kick your guitar used to give the rhythm. Maybe even take over for Joe until he comes back?"

"Thanks for asking, Bobby, but I'm going to be too busy trying to find Joe."

"Yeah, I guess so," he said in a resigned voice.

I rolled the sheet music he had given me and stuffed it in my suit coat. The mess Joe had left the band in depressed me and I decided to have a couple of drinks at the bar to bolster my ebbing spirits. Joe had to be in deep trouble to leave his band in such a lurch. He lived for his band. He wouldn't disappear unless it was a matter of life or death. I gulped the rest of my drink and asked the bartender, "Boots in his office?"

"Yeah, end of the hall," he replied without looking up. He reached under the bar and pressed a buzzer to alert Boots of a visitor come-a-calling.

I walked down the hallway to the last door and knocked. Sam the Barber opened up the door and snickered, "Well look who's here, the gumshoe."

A thatch of black hair topped Boots' cylindrical head, as if someone had put a wig on a can. Below his broad forehead, creased like a washboard, squinty black eyes framed a mashed-in nose, and even white teeth shone brightly through his permanent five o'clock shadow. His thick neck was set on a muscular square body. The spell in the pen didn't appear to have done him any harm.

Sam's partner, Tom, was leaning against the near wall. Gale was sitting in a chair opposite Boots. He dismissed her with a curt wave of his hand. Obediently, she stood and turned to leave.

"Isn't this a cozy setting," I said. "All it lacks is a fireplace."

Gale let out a small nervous laugh. "Everything was just a big mistake, Mr. Verriet." She motioned with her eyes to let me know there was more to it than what she was letting on as she passed me on her way out of the office.

Sam frisked me. "He's clean," he declared before I assumed the chair Gale had vacated.

"The last time I saw your boys was in my office. They broke in, cracked me on the skull, and left with Gale. Now you're all one big happy family," I added snidely.

Boots gave me a big smile, "Like the lady said, it was all a misunderstanding. I thought she took something that didn't belong to her. I was wrong."

"I owe your boys," I growled.

"They were protecting my interests," he said innocuously, spreading his hands on top of his desk. "I'll make it up to you, Verriet. I'd like to hire you to find Joe." He opened his desk drawer, fanned out five C-notes on top of his desk, and pushed them toward me.

"I already have a client. Besides, I was thinking you might already know Joe's whereabouts."

"Me? How dumb can you get? Would I be hiring you if I did?"

I ignored his jibe. "Why do you want to find Joe?"

"Jeez, you are dumb. He's my band leader, why else?"

"Because it stinks, that's why. There's more to it than you're shelling out. Don't insult my intelligence and deny it."

He gave my outburst a couple seconds of thought. "Let's just say Joe disappeared the same time something of mine went missing. I want to find him and ask him if he knows anything about it."

"You want to be a little more specific?"

"You find Joe and earn an easy five hundred more on top of this—call it a retainer," he said, moving the money closer to me.

"Uh-uh. Like I said, I've already got a client," I repeated and stood. Sam and Tom looked at Boots, he nodded, and they stepped aside for me to leave.

Gale sat at the bar with a drink, waiting for me as I came around the corner. She gave me a prodigious gander at her shapely pins sheathed in silk stockings.

I drifted to a stop at the stool next to her. "Boots agrees with you. He says it was all just a big misunderstanding. The next thing you'll tell me is I'm only imagining the stitches in my head."

She gave me a look as if indulging a child. "I finally convinced Boots that Joe didn't leave anything in that horn case except the note. Joe must have something Boots wants badly. You've got to find Joe before Boots does. I'm worried sick over him."

She didn't appear very worried when I walked in on their cozy meeting a few minutes ago.

"I'm working on it," I said noncommittally. "Anything else you want to tell me?"

She moved closer. I could feel the warmth of her body and smell her perfume. She wore a low-cut fringed black flapper dress. When she leaned over and gave me a good look, she whispered, "Find Joe and I'll be very grateful, Nick," and then settled back, breathed deeply, and gave me a knowing, sensuous smile that reminded me of a praying mantis about to eat her mate. "I better get ready for my show. Are you going to stick around?"

"I've got some work to do, but maybe you can convince me to stay awhile, sweet-cheeks," I said as I put my arm around her waist and pulled her undulant curves to my steerage.

"Stay and I'll sing you a special number later," she said breathlessly.

"You've convinced me," I said and planted my kisser on hers. She quivered against me, and returned my kiss, sending a charge of steam through my pipes. When she pulled her yielding softness away, I told her I'd see her later and legged it outside.

At my apartment, I placed the music sheets Bobby had given me on my work table, poured myself a tall glass of Old Granddad on the rocks, and sat down to see what ideas gramps stirred in my clockworks.

Boots is playing me. He isn't as interested in finding Joe as he is in recovering whatever is missing. Whatever it is, Boots thinks it was in the horn case. It could be anything. Does Joe have it? He must have, otherwise why has he skipped. But why run off with something if it's so hot? Maybe he didn't know what he had until it was too late. Too late for what? Too dangerous? Too incriminating?

Any written records Boots keeps will probably be enough to land him back in prison. But Joe wouldn't care about Boots' books, not enough to take them. He's too smart for that. And I can't imagine Joe purposely taking anything that would put him in a position where he has to go into hiding. Everything adds up to Joe not knowing what he had until it was too late to return it to Boots with impunity. That means it might be Boots' books. What else makes sense? But how could he take Boots' books and not know what they were? No, it can't be about books. I was back to zero.

Then there was Gale. *Was the affair in my office staged? If so, it was for my benefit, but why did she and Boots set it up? The only thing I'm sure of is Gale isn't telling me the whole truth. She claims to be worried about Joe. Is she having an affair with him?*

I remembered how Teri's feathers ruffled at the mention of Joe's singer. *Does she suspect Joe of having an affair? Oddly, the only person not looking for what's missing is Teri. Moreover, she doesn't exactly seem to want Joe back.*

I finished my drink and decided to begin with her again tomorrow. Maybe she'd think of something helpful with the right prodding. Maybe she was only pretending to want us to get back together. On the other hand, maybe I simply wanted to see her again and find out if fire is hot.

Continuing my mental perambulations, I considered what I learned from the band. *What about the new band member who acted edgy when I asked him about Joe? He plays tenor sax—was it his case Gale displayed in my office? Why? If I assume the whole shebang was staged, it means Boots wants me to become involved in something. Why and what? The obvious answer to the 'why' part of the question is that he is setting me up.*

A sudden chill crept up my spine as I considered the 'what' part of the question. *If this is a setup, it's for murder—Joe's murder. If someone killed Joe, Boots knows I'm the ideal candidate for the hot seat in Cook County Jail once the police dig into my past with Joe and Teri. The D.A. won't look beyond the fact I possess a motive, means, and opportunity. The hell of it is there isn't a damn thing I can do to change the past. If Joe's been iced, I'll rise to the top of the cop's most-likely-to-have-committed-bumpery list without help from Boots or anyone else.*

Chapter Five

Tuesday

I woke up late the next morning reticent to begin my day. As I lay in bed, my thoughts wandered, but always returned to Teri no matter how hard I tried to concentrate on other aspects of the case. Teri possessed the ineffable ability, like no other woman, to pry under my thick skin. I could still smell her after her shower; see her glistening tanned face, short raven black hair, and those beautiful dark brown eyes. My yearning for her tugged on my heartstrings until my chest ached and my pulse raced. *Why didn't I feel bad when she told me she was still interested?* "Stop the self-analysis," I said aloud and hauled my carcass out of bed.

After a lazy shower and shave, I dressed and strolled to the diner in the next block. It was the first day of summer; the sun was out, not a cloud in the sky. I wolfed a stack of wheats and washed them down with a large glass of orange juice chased with copious cups of coffee.

My office was six blocks away on Michigan Avenue. I had a one-room affair with a small anteroom and coat closet on the fifth floor of the Meyer Building with a nice view of the Art Museum down the street and Lake Michigan in the distance. My worn shoe leather made a slapping sound like a fast order cook pounding a two-bit steak as I trod the marble hallway. The answering service I shared with the other one-person enterprises on my floor was around the corner from my office. Ruth worked the day shift.

"Hi Ruthie, any messages?" I asked when I poked my head into her small cubicle and kissed the back of her neck.

She jumped at my touch. "Nick, I thought you were in your office. No messages, but some guy called for you early this morning. Said he'd call back later. Hey, what happened to your head?"

"Slipped in the shower," I replied airily. I began to walk away when the impact of what Ruthie had said hit me. Turning around, I stuck my head back in her office.

"Why did you think I was in my office, Ruthie?"

"I thought I saw a shadow move behind your office door when I went to the ladies room."

"How long ago was that?"

"Oh, about an hour, I guess."

"Thanks, kiddo," I said and left.

I slipped off my shoes, crept silently to my office, and listened at the door. No sounds were audible and no shadows appeared through the frosted glass. Slowly I turned the doorknob. The door wasn't locked and I eased it open. Somebody had ransacked my office; all my file cabinet drawers were open and emptied of their contents. Papers were strewn everywhere. My coat closet's contents lay in a heap.

With a curse, I slipped my shoes back on and set to work. I began to reorganize the paperwork and refile case histories into the cabinets. As best I could make out, only my address book was missing. I had a hunch I knew what the burglar was after. Two hours later I still had a mess, but an organized mess.

I went to the men's room to wash the dust off my hands before I returned to my office. Kicking back in my chair, feet up on my desk and phone in hand, I dialed the Marcus' number.

"Teri, Nick. Have you heard from Joe yet?"

"No. Anything on your end?"

"Nothing, but I'd like to ask you a couple more questions. Can you meet me for lunch?"

"Why don't you come here and I'll fix us something?" she asked solicitously.

"Sounds good, but I need to be at a meeting downtown early this afternoon," I fibbed. "Can you come downtown? We can meet at the Berghoff." She sounded disappointed, but agreed to meet me in half an hour.

I closed up my office and told Ruthie I'd be out for the rest of the day. Tension began to build in me like an over-wound

Victrola as I walked to the restaurant. Rounding the corner of Adams Street, I glimmed Teri as she approached the front door and went inside. A few seconds later, my heart pounding, I pushed the revolving door and entered the dark wood-paneled entryway. Teri got up from one of the small anteroom side benches, gave me a big smile followed by a light kiss on the cheek. Her familiar perfume surrounded me in delicate redolent waves of freshness.

Seated at a table near the back, a waiter immediately came over to take our order. Teri ordered wiener schnitzel with spätzle and I ordered their sausage platter with red cabbage. We both indulged in their special home-brewed root beer.

"Isn't that the same thing you used to order when you first brought me here?" she asked with a grin.

"Yeah, I guess I'm a creature of habit. Besides, I know a good thing when I taste it." A feeling of uneasiness stirred in my grey matter as we started to slip into our old easy rapport.

"I remember that about you," she said coyly, reaching out and touching my hand.

Just like that, she had me. "Before I forget, thanks for joining me," I said hastily. "I've been thinking of Joe, where he might have disappeared to, and I think he probably left town. Does he have any relatives around or a favorite haunt?"

She searched my face. "He isn't close to any relatives. He likes a few places where he's played more than others, but I couldn't pick one out over the rest."

"Does he ever get away by himself or go someplace special with the guys?"

"Of course! Why didn't I think of it sooner?" she answered excitedly. "He bought a small place, a cabin, on a lake up in Wisconsin a couple of years ago. He goes fishing up there every year. I went with him a couple times, but there wasn't much to do but fish, so thankfully he started going with Tom and some of the guys."

"Who's Tom and how does Joe know him?"

"Tom Harris. He manages a resort by Lake Geneva. He used to book Joe's band for part of the tourist season and that's how they met. Joe hasn't played there for a while, but they've stayed in touch and still use the cabin for their annual outings."

"Do you think Joe could be at the cabin?"

"Sure. Now that I think about it, I'd bet on it. I feel so stupid for not thinking about it earlier," she said in exasperation.

"Don't be too hard on yourself. We all tend to overlook the obvious. Do you feel like taking a ride up there with me after lunch—after my business meeting?" I quickly amended as I remembered my earlier fib.

"I'd love to," she said all too willingly.

Chapter Six

We enjoyed the beautiful afternoon, warm with a slight breeze—perfect for cruising up north in my struggle buggy. Teri snuggled up on the passenger side like a cat sitting on a window cushion in the warm embracing sunshine. She had on a white peasant blouse tied in a knot at the waist and a pair of sporting knickers. Her outfit made it hard for me to concentrate on the road.

Traffic was heavy until we reached the far North Side. Another thirty minutes and I crossed the border into Wisconsin. Occasionally, my work took me across the state line, although outside of Illinois my license wasn't worth the paper it was printed on. I'd have to tread lightly up north and avoid the local gendarmes at all costs.

As I turned off the main highway, I spotted a shadow, a large black sedan following about five hundred yards back. The car slowed when I took the turn-off. He kept enough distance to disappear from my rearview mirror on the curves. I drove leisurely to prevent him from knowing I knew he was there. We went a few more miles before Teri directed me to a winding country road on our left.

Ten minutes later, we took a hairpin turn onto a narrow sandy road. If she hadn't cautioned me about the sharp turn, I would have missed it as my tail was likely to do. An old faded white wooden sign with slats graced the road entranceway—cabin owners' names painted in black on the markers. I pulled over to the side, and climbed out of the car to Teri's bewildered look. I grabbed the wooden slat with Joe's name on it and ripped it off the supporting boards, tossing it into the brush.

When I scrambled back in the car, Teri asked, "What was that all about?"

"Somebody is tailing us and I don't want to make it too easy for him."

"How could he know we were coming up here?"

"Maybe he didn't. He may have been watching one of us before we met for lunch. I'm sure he'll miss that last turn unless he already knows about the cabin. We'll give him some time just in case. Who knows? Maybe it's Joe."

She was silent as I eased the car into low gear and maneuvered my buggy around the ruts and rocks lining the single-lane dirt road. Joe's cabin was set a few hundred feet back from the road in a grassy clearing. I spotted another cabin a quarter mile or so further down the lane. A brilliant blue lake glimmered off in the distance. I drove down the grassy embankment studded with dandelions and parked next to the cabin, a small solid log job that needed re-chinking. The smell of the surrounding pine trees filled the air.

We climbed out and looked around. Someone had been here recently. I pointed out the car tire impressions in the grass to Teri. She cautiously opened the screen door, tried the knob, found it locked and rapped on the pine inner door. There was no response so she tried again. No answer. We walked around to the lakeside and peered in through the windows.

Halfway between Joe's cabin and the lake were small structures set in two rows about fifteen feet between each pair. They looked like dollhouses on stilts. I counted twelve of them.

"What the hell are those?" I asked pointing to the little huts.

Teri laughed lightly. "They're for the bees."

"Bees?"

"Yeah, Joe likes honey. He claims it helps his playing, so he keeps bees."

"I'll be damned," I mumbled. Joe, an apiarist—you never can tell about some guys.

"I don't have a key. Can you pick the lock?" Teri asked when we discovered the porch door locked as well.

"I could if I had my tools with me. I guess we'll have to enter the old fashioned way," I exclaimed as I untied one shoe and slipped it off. Holding the toe, I tapped the heel against a window to the left of the door. The pane was old and brittle and broke easily. I reached in, unfastened the latch and slid the window up.

31

If Joe was here, he wasn't dead to judge by the musty odor that assailed my nostrils.

"Think you can fit through there?"

"No problem."

I made a cradle for her foot by lacing my fingers together. She placed one foot on my hands and lifted her other leg over the sill. "Watch the glass," I cautioned.

She bent forward, her knickers riding up on her shapely gams as she squeezed her torso through the opening and pulled her trailing leg in behind her. A couple of seconds later she opened the door and I joined her inside.

The cabin had a small cozy living area and kitchen. The screened-in porch sat on the lakeside with a tiny bathroom set off to the side. Two small bedrooms were on the right; faded drapes hanging from small rods across each doorway provided a modicum of privacy. A wood-burning stove and table with a checkered tablecloth completed the north woods retreat.

"Has Joe come up here this year?"

"Not that I know of."

"Well somebody's been here recently. There's smudges in the dust," I said as I went over to the ice box to look inside. "And there's fresh groceries," I added holding the door open for her to look.

"It must be Joe," she frowned.

"Does he ever let anyone else use the cabin?"

She wrinkled her forehead and said, "Maybe Tom. I'm not sure."

"I guess we wait around and see if anyone shows. From the tire tracks, someone's been here and left. I don't want to tip off our presence so I'm going to move my car to one of the cabins further down the lane. Meanwhile, see if Joe's stashed something to drink."

I parked behind the neighbor's garage so no one would lamp my flivver unless he drove past Joe's. I reached under the dash and removed my .45 special from its custom holder, and stuck it under my waistband. There was no sign of our earlier tail as I walked back to Joe's cabin. Teri proudly pushed a tall glass of scotch on the rocks in my hand when I entered the kitchen.

"Typical Joe," she remarked. "He's got more booze than food in the cupboard."

"A man after my own heart," I grinned.

We gravitated to the screened-in porch and made ourselves comfortable on an old beat-up sofa. A pileated woodpecker echoed through the trees in search of insects, and an occasional fish surfaced, sending ripples across the lake in ever widening concentric circles. I had forgotten how tranquil it was up in the north woods.

Teri, eyes bright, must have shared my sentiment. She nestled by my side and we silently took in the beautiful serenity as we sipped our drinks. When I slipped into the kitchen to get us a refill, I spied a coat rack with dirty white overhauls hanging on the bathroom door.

"What's that?" I asked, motioning at the coat rack with my head as I handed Teri her drink.

"Joe's bee suit. He wears it when he collects honey. There's a headpiece, too."

"Just goes to show you, I guess. You can know a guy almost you're whole life and still not know everything there is to know about him," I remarked.

"Have you ever had fresh honey?" she asked as I eased back on the sofa next to her.

"No, but I've known a few fresh honeys."

She poked me in the ribs. "I bet you have," she admonished and repositioned herself to rest her head in my lap, looking up at me with her exquisite orbs.

I swallowed hard. The alcohol and pine-scented air swirled through my head. Her eyes fluttered, she licked her lips, said softly, "Kiss me, Nick," and pulled me to her waiting lips.

When my mouth touched hers, a warm tingling sensation raced up my spine to the back of my head. I shivered involuntarily, and mashed my mouth on hers as my hand rode up her side to her breast. I smashed her yielding curves against me until she trembled in my grasp. When I let go, both of us were breathing deeply. She took my glass, set it on the floor, and shifted her sleek curves to better fit my nooks and crannies. We kissed again and she responded to my every move. Without a word, I lifted her in my arms and carried her into one of the bedrooms.

Afterwards, lying in the crook of my arm, she moaned huskily, "It's always been the best with us, hasn't it, Nick?"

"Yeah," I conceded hoarsely. "No matter how hard I've tried, I could never get you out of my blood. I think I hated you for it."

"I know," she said softly. "That's the real reason why you stopped coming around, isn't it?"

"Yeah," I admitted.

She leaned over me and gave me a light kiss. "Nick, I've been thinking about leaving Joe for some time. I know now I should have left long ago. Maybe we can make up for lost time."

"I'm willing to try, but let's not complicate things more than they are right now. After I find Joe, we'll talk. Meantime, I'm getting hungry."

She groaned. "Why am I not surprised? Get dressed and help me open some cans in the kitchen."

There was dried venison in the icebox. When I asked Teri about it, she said besides fishing, Joe hunted with his friends. Another surprise—first, fishing, then beekeeping, and now hunting. *What else didn't I know about him?*

I managed to make a tasty stew out of the venison simmered in red wine. We had canned beans and peaches on the side and split the rest of the bottle of wine by candlelight. By the time we finished, it was approaching ten-thirty and there was still no sign of Joe.

I helped Teri with the few dishes. We had another scotch on the porch and listened to the bullfrogs' serenade, intermittently interrupted by a loon's cry. Eventually, the chill night air pushed us inside. After we tidied up the bedroom, we started back for the city. As a precaution, I kept my head lamps off until I hit the main highway.

When I pulled up to Teri and Joe's place, it was after one in the morning. I walked her to her front door. She put her key in the lock, turned the handle and with the door partly opened, froze. I glanced over her shoulder. The living room looked like a proverbial Midwest tornado had raced through it.

"Stay back," I whispered in her ear and gently pulled her to the side of the door. I reached for my gun, pivoted my tonnage through the door quickly, and fanned the room from left to right. A cool draft was coming from the rear of the house. I walked to the kitchen and discovered a broken window in the back door. I searched the bedrooms before I proceeded to the basement. Finding nothing but a mess, I searched the garage. The side door had been jimmied open. Whoever had broken in had done a thorough but frantic search. I walked to the front of the house and told Teri it was safe to enter.

"Look at this place!" she said assessing the damage as she walked from room to room.

"My office got the same treatment yesterday. We better call the cops."

"No," Teri said putting her hand on my arm as I reached for the phone. "What are the cops going to do but make a report? They can't accomplish anything that you can't. Nothing's been taken as far as I can tell. It'll take me quite a while to clean up, but it will help me keep my mind off things."

"Maybe you better make sure nothing's missing," I suggested.

She gave a sorrowful smile, and said, "There's nothing worth taking and my check book and money are in my purse."

"Is there anything you want me to do?"

She nodded with a solemn look, "Spend the night, Nick. I'd feel safer."

"What if Joe shows up?"

"I already told you how I feel. We'll deal with Joe whenever we have to," she replied earnestly.

"Sure, Teri," I said. I didn't tell her I thought there was little chance of Joe ever showing up again.

Chapter Seven

Wednesday

Teri slept, curled by my side, while I thought about everything that had taken place over the last two days. The luminescent hands on my watch showed half past six when I finally slipped out of bed. Teri looked so good, she made me want to stay, but I reminded myself the sooner I cleared up matters concerning Joe, the sooner I'd never have to leave her again. Though I had scarcely slept, I felt great as I mulled over the prospect of Teri and I together again. As I jumped into my bucket of bolts. Being with her made me feel whole.

I arrived at my apartment to discover it had been ransacked as well. An inspection of the lock revealed someone with the right tools had opened it, just like my office. *Did the same person break into my office, my apartment, and Teri's? If so, why did he pick the locks on my office and apartment, but smash a window and jimmy a door to gain entry at Teri's? The coincidence is too great for the events to be unrelated. Maybe two different people are responsible. Boots' boys?*

I contemplated the possibilities as I shaved and showered. For breakfast, I ate scrambled eggs and downed four cups of coffee with a couple slices of dry toast. After cleaning the dishes, I began to tackle my apartment's clean-up job beginning with the furniture. Once I finished with the big items, I decided the small stuff could wait until later after a thorough check revealed nothing missing. I tucked my rodney in its holster, and headed out.

I picked up my laundry at the cleaners before going to the office. Ruthie's cute smile, emphasized by a slight overbite and her carrot-orange hair, immediately brightened my day. "Any messages, hot stuff?"

She looked in my portal, pulled out a wad of papers and sifted through them. "They're all from the same guy who called yesterday. He still didn't leave his name or number. And there's one from Butters," she said extracting his message from the pile and handing it to me. "He wants you to call him."

"If that other guy calls again, tell him I'll be in my office at noon today," I instructed her and walked to my office. I grabbed the phone on my desk and dialed the number Teri had given me to reach Joe's fishing buddy, Tom. When he answered, I briefly explained who I was and why I was calling.

"You say Joe's missing?"

"That's right. I'm calling all his friends to see if they might have seen him lately or had contact with him."

"Last time Joe and I talked was a couple of weeks ago. We made plans for our annual Fourth of July fishing outing."

"When was the last time you were at his cabin?"

"Last fall when we went hunting," he said. "Is there anything I can do to help? Joe's a good guy. I hate to think he's in any trouble."

"There's nothing for the time being, but if something comes up I'll remember your offer. If you hear from Joe, tell him to call me immediately." I gave him my office and home number before I cradled the earpiece.

I locked up my office and walked over to Frankie's. Frankie was at his usual station tending bar when I walked in. Butters must have told him to keep an eye out for me because Frankie nodded and motioned towards the back room when he eyed me. Butters was having a cup of java and reading a racing form when I rapped on the back room doorframe. "Who won the third race at Hawthorne two weeks ago from Friday?"

"Hey, Nick. I was just thinkin' 'bout you. And it was Brown-eyed Girl," he said with a grin.

Frankie walked in, put a mug in front of me, and filled it with coffee before he topped off Butters' cup. I thanked him and waited until he left us alone to find out what Butters had dug up.

"What have you got for me?"

"I know how Boots scrounged the moolah so fast after he got outta da pen. He put da big squeeze on Freddie McClanahan," he said matter-of-factly, "and when Freddie didn't bite, he iced him and took over his numbers operation—lock, stock, and barrel."

"Why would Boots want in on the numbers action? He's always run joints and women."

"Must be expandin'. Freddie wasn't da only one. After he chilled Freddie, he squeezed out two more operators. Da word is he's makin' a play to sew up da numbers racket in Chi."

"Something's odd about all this," I ventured.

"Don't discard the moolah involved, Nick. Runnin' numbers is big business these days, especially on da South Side."

"Maybe, but something's fishy. You find out anything about Joe?"

He shook his head, "Man, that guy's vanished into thin air. Nobody knows a thing. Ya want I should keep askin' around?"

"Yeah, but watch your back. I picked up a tail yesterday. Somebody is looking real hard for something Joe supposedly stole from Boots."

I told Butters about my office and apartment ransacking. I also related the details of Joe and Teri's home invasion.

"Ya wanna know what I think?"

"Always open to speculation, pally."

"I think Joe got his hot mitts on Boots' numbers books. Maybe he didn't know what he had at da time and after he realized it, it was too late. Boots knows Joe has his books and Joe knows Boots won't let him off da hook. He's between a rock and a hard place and doesn't know which way to turn. He's hidin' out, more nervous dan a cat tryin' to bury shit on an ice pond."

"Uh-huh. That's sort of the way I figure it, too. Most of it fits."

"Damned straight it fits," Butters acknowledge, bobbing his head up and down vigorously.

Frankie returned to refill our mugs. I handed him a couple bills and he returned to the bar to wait on his other patrons.

"Let's suppose your theory is right," I offered. "Why didn't Joe go to the cops when he realized he had Boots' books?"

"Maybe he's tryin' to figure a way to leverage things with Boots."

I shook my head. "Could be, but I don't think so. That's not the Joe I know."

Butters shrugged his shoulders, and said, "Or maybe he figures Boots will get to him before da cops can do anythin' with da information. Boots is smart. Maybe he used a code system. Remember Johnny D, da old bootlegger? He was smart like dat. The cops never did crack his code and he got off with only a couple of misdemeanors."

"Or maybe Joe is worried about his career," I adjoined. "If he goes to the cops, he'd be in a tight spot. Word will get out he was the one who fingered Boots. Most of the clubs are mob owned and the other club owners will be sure to blackball him and his band."

"Hey, I never thought of dat angle," Butters effused, "I think ya hit da nail on da head, buddy."

We bantered back and forth for another twenty minutes before I left a fiver on the table and thanked him for the information.

Back in my office, I searched amongst my files for those on Freddie McClanahan and a few of his cronies to reacquaint myself with Chicago's numbers business. Nothing I had connected them to Boots. Finished, I put a call into the diner down the street and asked them to send up a couple of sandwiches before I continued going through the files.

I was still drawing a blank when my phone rang. I barely said, "Hello," into the mouthpiece before Joe blurted out, "Nick. Thank god. I've been trying to reach you for a day and a half."

"Likewise. It's good to hear your voice," I responded automatically. "I was getting worried."

"Nick. I need your help. I'm in a terrible jam. Can you meet me right away?" he pleaded.

"I'm on my way as soon as you tell me where you're at."

He gave me an address on the near South Side about a dozen blocks in from the lake. I told him I'd be there as soon as possible and hung up. On my way out, I bumped into the delivery boy from the deli. I fished a bill out of my pocket, tossed it to him and grabbed the bag out of his hand.

"Keep the change," I hollered as I rushed to the elevator.

I hustled over to the municipal garage, told the attendant to fetch my jalopy in one minute for two bits. He made it with five seconds to spare scorching what smelled like two bucks worth of rubber off my tires en route. During the drive, I wolfed down the sandwiches and cursed myself for not getting something to drink.

Exactly twenty-three minutes later, I pulled up to a dilapidated dirty gray house. The address numbers, 21032, hung at despairing angles on weathered clapboard siding next to a rickety front door. The screen door swung from a single rusted hinge and the porch sagged in the middle. A dog next door yelped in response to my knock. When I turned, I saw a dirty-yellow mongrel chained to a tree, and out of the corner of my eye, I spotted a guy walking toward me across the street at the far end of the block. I stepped back to take a better gander at him when the sound of creaking floorboards and the rattle of the doorknob refocused my attention.

Joe peered through the cracked door. He looked like he'd been on a week-long bender. He reached an arm out, grabbed my coat sleeve, and pulled me stumbling headlong into the house. Then he stuck his head out the door and looked around furtively before he closed it tight.

His eyes were red road maps, his hair matched his disheveled clothes. He hadn't shaved in days. Without so much as a howdy-do, he nudged me into the parlor where a couple of moth-eaten chairs kept company with a worn-out sofa.

An empty bottle of hooch was on a badly stained side table. Other empty bottles lined the floor under the table. I sat in one of the chairs as Joe fumbled with a cigarette. I let him take a few puffs while he wore grooves pacing the floor. The floor didn't seem to mind.

I studied him without saying anything. My silence seemed to make him more nervous.

Abruptly, he stopped pacing and blurted out, "Nick, I need help bad. I want you to return something I took from Boots."

"Sure, Joe. What did you take?"

"First, you gotta agree to get Boots off my back. I've thought everything through from every angle and I've decided there's only one way to go. You've gotta convince him that I didn't know what I was doing. It was all a mistake. Tell him I'll do whatever he wants to make amends—just as long as he lets me off the hook."

"Ab-so-lute-ly. I'll do whatever it takes to help you and you know it."

He picked up the bottle from the table without realizing it was empty. Swearing, he tossed it aside and grabbed a fresh one from a buffet set against the far wall. Tearing open the seal, he upended the bottle and gulped a big slug, wiped his mouth with the back of his hand and offered it to me. When I turned down the drink, he took another long pull.

"Look, Nick. You're the only guy I can trust. That's why I called you. But I'm not asking you to do this for free. I'll pay you for your time. I owe you that much," he said and reached in his pants pocket. He pulled out a handful of crumpled bills and handed them to me. I counted thirteen twenty dollar bills. I stood up and stiffly shoved them into his shirt pocket with distaste.

"Let's start at the beginning," I prodded. "Who owns this place and what did you take?"

"Harry Jeffers owns this dump. You remember him, don't you?"

"Yeah, the old blues man."

"Uh-huh. He gave me a key for part-time players and guys passin' through town," he explained.

"Now get to the meat. What did you take?"

Silence permeated the room like fog rolling over a riverbank until the insistent noise of the neighbor's dog barking snapped Joe's attention back to me. He absently noted his cigarette had burned down to his fingers, dropped it on the floor to join its comrades and reached for another. Finding his pack empty, he looked at me.

"Sorry, you know I don't smoke," I said in response to his searching look.

"Let me grab a pack from the kitchen," he said and left. The seconds turned into minutes. I wondered what was taking him so long. Then it hit me. The neighbor's dog had suddenly stopped barking which meant whomever it had barked at was no longer within sight. I sprang off the sofa and rushed into the kitchen. I heard a rush of air a moment before my head exploded in light followed by searing pain. *Not again.* Tiny pinpricks of light faded into darkness like dissolving fireworks and then all was quiet.

I came to in slow rolling waves. I unsteadily gained my feet and went to the parlor calling Joe's name—no answer. I grabbed the bottle of whiskey, held my breath and took a couple of swigs. My hands hurt like hell. When I set the bottle down, I looked at my knuckles—bruised and scraped raw. Whoever conked me must have ground their heels on them. I felt my way back to the kitchen where I chased the booze with some cool tap water and doused my head to clear the cobwebs. Thankfully, the skin wasn't broken and there was no blood, only a golf ball sized lump behind my right ear. The water felt better on my head and hands than it did in my stomach.

A trail of blood led off to the bottom of a stairway. I hugged the walls and climbed the rickety stairs, stopping a couple of times to catch my breath. Upstairs were three small bedrooms. I found Joe in the third one. Someone had secured him to a chair with a belt and some torn sheets. His face was an unrecognizable bloody, pulpy mess. Both eyes were swollen shut and his jaw must have been broken to judge from the odd angle his mouth hung open. I felt for a pulse in vain.

His empty wallet lay in the corner. Then I remembered the money Joe had tried to force on me. I searched his pockets. Empty. Whoever killed him had quite a payday. I did a quick search of the premises, but the killer had left no visible traces behind and I didn't find anything belonging to Boots.

Downstairs, I grabbed the bottle of booze I had handled and tucked it into my coat. I wiped down everything I had touched and beat it. From the artwork on my knuckles, it looked like somebody had set me up for a murder rap. I stopped once on the way back to the city to toss the bottle into a trash receptacle and to phone the police. When the desk sergeant answered, I gave the address, mentioned a murder, and hung up. I went back to my car and hadn't driven more than a block before I heard a police siren.

I drove straight to Teri's. When she opened the door, she took one look at my face and knew something was wrong. She took my hand and led me to the sofa in the living room. After we both were seated, she tremulously asked, "It's Joe, isn't it?"

"Yeah, I found him. He's dead." Just like that. Quick.

She let out a small gasp, leaned forward, clutched her knees and began to rock back and forth as she cried. I put my arm around her and felt like a heel. Sure, I wanted her all to myself, but not this way. I'd rather have Joe alive and mad at me for taking Teri back.

She must have read my mind, "I feel so rotten, Nick. Here we were making love yesterday and today Joe's dead. I never imagined he was really in serious danger. What a fool I've been. I should have been out there looking for him with you. How can I ever forgive myself?"

I didn't tell her the details of Joe's death and I didn't have an answer for her. I removed my arm and we sat in silence. Finally, I stood up and said flatly, "I'll find Joe's killer, Teri. Maybe if I bring his killer to justice, we can both find some answers. I better hightail it, the cops will be here soon. Try to act shocked when they tell you the news. I don't want them to know I found his body."

She nodded feebly. I turned and left her staring into space, tears running down her cheeks.

Chapter Eight

Thunderhead clouds filled the sky as I drove back downtown. By the time I reached Boot's place, the rain was coming down in wind-driven sheets. I stamped my feet on the entrance doormat, walked straight past the bar area, down the hall, and into Boots' office without knocking. Tom had his gun drawn before I closed the door behind me. I automatically held up my arms for Sam to relieve me of my rod. His hands showed no signs of a beating and a glance at Tom's revealed the same. I reminded myself they were pros with a lot of experience. Their knuckles weren't cut or bruised, but that didn't mean they weren't responsible for Joe's death. Pros often used gloves.

Boots lounged in his big leather chair behind a huge oak desk that badly needed varnish. Papers lay strewn across the top. Names and numbers written in neat columns dotted the papers. Boots grabbed up the papers, stuffed them into a drawer, and motioned for me to sit down opposite him.

"I found Joe."

Boots' eyes shifted up to meet mine in an unwavering stare. My news didn't elicit any reaction from him. If his boys had killed Joe, he was a better actor than I gave him credit for being.

"Where is he?" he asked anxiously.

"He was shacked up in a place on the near South Side."

"Was?" he asked stoically.

"Yeah. He was dead when I found him," I lied.

Boots' eyes hardened. "Did you notify the cops?"

"Yep."

"Did you search the place?"

"Uh-huh. There wasn't anything there. Either his killer took the goods, or Joe hid beforehand whatever it was he took. Now are you going to tell me what *it* is?"

Ignoring my question, Boots asked challengingly, "How do I know you didn't find it?"

"You don't," I rasped, "but think about this. First, if I had found something, would I be here telling you about it? Second, I don't even know what the hell I'm looking for. Third, Joe was my friend. He went missing. I figured he was in trouble so I tried to help him," I paused before adding pugnaciously, "that's the long and short of it."

Tom shifted uneasily, and Sam repeatedly flicked his barber's straight razor open and closed while Boots' eyes drilled into me. I suddenly wished I did smoke so I had something to do with my idle hands.

"Ya got any ideas?"

"I've got a lot of ideas, Boots."

We sat and stared at each other in silence while he clipped off the end of a cigar and held a lighter to the tip, rolling the cigar deftly between manicured fingers. He appeared to reach some conclusion because with a nod he reached in his top desk drawer. I half expected him to pull a rod on me. Instead, he pulled out a wad of Clevelands and placed five neat little stacks in front of me.

"For expenses. I'm hiring you. If you return my case intact," he added, "there'll be another hundred in it for you. How's that?"

"Lousy. This whole thing stinks and you can keep your stinking money."

He gave me a gallows look and I heard Sam move beside me. Boots fought for inner control, his face twisting into an evil sneer. He looked down at his desktop for a few seconds and when his gaze returned to me, his face bore its earlier blank countenance.

A blank look, coupled with silence, supposedly makes people nervous, and when people are nervous they often talk and reveal things they normally wouldn't. If Boots was exercising this technique on me, I wasn't buying it. I contemplated the furnishings, even turned in my chair to stare at Tom. He shifted his feet uneasily under my scrutiny, before I shifted my attention to Sam who, with a hungry look, ran an index finger along his blade.

Boots finally broke the silence. "Look, Verriet, you find the goods and who killed Joe. When you find out, you call and I'll send the boys to fetch the goods. I get what's mine and I give you two hundred more. You find out who killed Joe and I'll throw in another hundred. That's all you gotta do."

I thought about his proposition. I needed the dough and finding Joe fulfilled my obligations to both Gale and Teri. *Why not take Boots' money for the job?* After all, I intended to find Joe's killer anyway. The angles played in my favor, so I scooped up the hundred before he changed his mind.

"Deal."

"Thatta boy," Boots said and nodded at Sam to open the door in dismissal. Without another word, I took my leave.

I found Gale sipping a drink at the bar. I joined her, signaled to the bartender, and when he approached us, said, "Rye," to his questioning look.

Gale gave me the cold shoulder. When the bartender served up my drink, I said, "Cheers," and held up my glass to hers.

"I thought you said you were going to stay and hear me sing the other night," she snipped.

"Sorry about that, but something came up with Joe," I said half-truthfully.

"Did you find him?" she asked with big eyes.

"Yeah, he's dead. Somebody gave him the beating of his life."

Her eyes flashed, she drew in a breath that tested both the tensile strength of her dress and my eyeball sockets. "What about the money?" she whispered anxiously.

I tried to keep shock from registering on my face. This was the first mention I'd heard of any missing money. I shook my head.

"What about Boots?" she asked with a frightened look.

"I thought you told me the whole affair was all a big mistake," I challenged. Suddenly it occurred to me she had never said anything about me returning the money she had given me at our first meeting. *Why hadn't I thought of it earlier?* I was off my game. Letting Teri under my skin was going to cost me dearly if I wasn't more careful.

"It *was* a mistake," she insisted, "but I still want you to find the money Joe took from Boots."

"That's news to me. You never mentioned Joe stole any money from Boots when you came to my office. Is that what you thought had been in the case?"

She blushed slightly and stammered, "I-I wasn't sh-sure . . . I c-could trust you. I figured you'd keep the money for yourself if I told you."

"Why the sudden faith?" I asked sharply.

She moved closer and whispered huskily, "I know you better now, and I'm a good judge of character. You find the money and we'll split it down the middle. Do we have a deal, big boy?"

"I already have another client, lambkins. Boots hired me to find his money after I told him about Joe."

Her face turned red and her lip curled. "I thought you were working for me!" she said and stamped her heel down on my foot.

"Ouch! Listen lady—"

"Oh! I'm sorry, Nick. I guess the news about Joe's death has me a little on edge," she said, adroitly changing tactics.

"Look, there's no way I'm keeping Boots' stolen money if I find it. Eventually he'd find out, and he'd get his money back with the vig paid in my blood. If you want to take your chances, you can have it all. And I've used up your retainer," I quickly added. "Your earlier payment barely covered my doctor's bill for the stitch work on my head. Against my better judgment, I'll keep on the case for you, but I'll need at least another fifty."

I told myself I shouldn't take them both on as clients, but this bunch certainly wasn't going to file any claims regarding my ethics. Besides, they were obviously playing me for a sucker, so I figured fair was fair.

She ran her fingers tenderly across my stitches. "Okay, lover." She smiled, reached under her dress and pulled out a small roll of money she must have secured with a garter. She paused a moment to give me a good glim of her sheathed stemwork.

"I always keep a little pin-money on me. Mother told me you never know when you might be left high and dry. She knew what she was talking about, too—high, but never dry, her whole life."

She peeled off five sawbucks, pressed close to me, put the money in my hand and clasped it against her bosom. She smelled of expensive perfume. I placed my other hand on her thigh and she let out a purr. *Why not?* I leaned over and kissed her. An ear-shattering crash shattered the moment.

I looked over to where the sound had emanated from and saw Bobby in a heated discussion with the edgy sax player. A couple of bandstands lay on the floor nearby.

Gale abruptly said, "Excuse me, Nick," and rushed over to the ruckus. She grabbed the sax player by the arm and he hauled off and slapped her. She stumbled away from him, her face a frozen mask. She grabbed his arm again, mumbled something in his ear, and pulled him to the back of the stage area.

I walked over to Bobby. "What's with the new guy?"

"My bad luck is running true. He's on the H-train and his source has dried up. He's hurting bad and is taking it out on everybody around him. If he doesn't score soon, I'm going to be out a tenor man."

"That explains why he was so touchy the last time I was here. I suppose my being a private dick didn't help either."

Bobby nodded. "Yeah, the kid's a great sax player, but unreliable as hell. On top of everything else, the bass player's wife is sick and he left town for a few days. I'm left with only the drummer for rhythm."

"I'm afraid I've got more bad news for you, Bobby."

He groaned. "Man, it don't rain but what it pours. Go ahead, lay it on me."

"Joe's not coming back."

Color drained from his face. "Dead?"

I nodded. "Murdered."

"Oh shit," he gasped and went over to one of the band chairs and sat down. He put his head in his hands. "Who'd want to kill Joe? He was the nicest guy in the world."

"I've got a couple of ideas," I said and straddled an adjacent chair. I glimmed Bobbie's distraught face and cut to the chase.

"Bobby, you need to take charge of the band. I'm sure it's what Joe would have wanted."

"Maybe," he frowned, "but I don't want to be a band leader— it's way too many headaches. Dealing with Chuck is more than I can take. I just want to go on being a player."

"Chuck is the new sax player?"

"Yeah. What the hell am I going to do? I need this gig, this band's the best gravy train I've had for a long time."

"Seems to me you and the boys need to find a new band leader. Joe had a solid reputation and so did his bands. Shouldn't be hard for you to find somebody willing to step in given the state of things. Stick with it for a few days and see what Boots wants to do. In the meantime, put some feelers out and ask the guys for potential candidates. Things will work out one way or the other. Life goes on no matter what happens. This, too, will pass."

"Yeah, so do kidney stones." Sadly shaking his head, he said resignedly, "I suppose you're right."

"One piece of advice, Bobby."

He looked up at me helplessly. "Yeah?"

"Might be smart to start putting feelers out for another gig, too. Don't ask why, call it a hunch."

I left him sitting frozen to his chair, staring off into space. My words seemed to have that effect on everybody lately.

Chapter Nine

At the end of each business day, Ruthie makes duplicates of my messages when I'm out and sticks them through my office door mail slot. She knows I keep irregular office hours, often stopping by in the middle of the night. This time the only thing I found on the floor when I reached my office was a life insurance advertisement. My life wasn't worth the cost of the premiums to anybody but me. Then I thought about Teri. She was the one person who could change my situation, so I tossed the flyer in my desk drawer and grabbed the phone. She answered on the fourth ring.

"Thought I'd call and see how you're doing."

"Thanks, Nick. I'm as good as can be expected, I guess. I had to go identify Joe's body. It was awful. I only recognized his clothes. Who would do such a thing to him?"

"I don't know, Teri, but I'll find out. How did you make out with the cops?"

"They asked me if I knew who killed Joe and I told them I had no idea," she replied in a faraway sounding voice. "I told them about him not coming home for the last few days. They asked why I didn't report him missing. I told them I had hired you to find Joe instead and they asked me a lot of questions about you. Then they asked me about Boots' nightclub and the house where they found Joe. I told them the truth. I hope I did okay."

"I'm sure you did fine. I'll handle the cops if they come around. Try to rest and get some sleep. I'll talk to you tomorrow," I said and hung up. I was all balled up. The strained undercurrent to our conversation made me restless, so I decided to lock up the office and walk over to Frankie's.

Butters was out and hadn't left any messages for me. I mounted a bar stool and shot the breeze with Frankie while I drank boilermakers. Somehow, the alcohol didn't help me forget my day and that old craving came back to haunt me—a desire to put a soft cushion between me and reality. Some place where I could escape all the pain of living and just float in a sea of insensate tupor. I fought down the feeling and had a couple more drinks until I was so numb I didn't care about a damn thing. Frankie flagged down a hack to take me home where I had another couple of drinks, collapsed on my living room sofa and fell asleep with my clothes on.

Chapter Ten

Thursday

My mouth tasted like a muddy cotton field and my head throbbed incessantly beneath my stitches. I applied an ice pack to the back of my head and dropped a teaspoon of aspirin powder into my cup of java until I felt like tackling the rest of the mess in my apartment. While I organized and cleaned, I thought about Joe's killer and the mad search for Boots' missing case.

Gale said the case contained money. I don't see any reason why Boots would hide that fact if money was taken from him. Taking money wouldn't have put Joe in such a panic, either. No, Gale has to be lying. Boots' missing materials are probably connected to his new numbers' venture, but why is Gale interested in numbers running? Is she working for one of the other numbers bosses? Or . . . maybe she's Boots' puppet— insurance to cover all the angles.

From experience, I knew the answer would surface as long as I didn't try to push too hard. With my nervous energy subsiding, I shaved and climbed in the shower. Dressed, and with a heightened determination to find Joe's killer, I flipped on my fedora and walked to my office, stopping to buy a *Times* from Jaunty John's corner newsstand.

When I entered the message center, Ruthie looked up, rolled her eyes towards my office and silently mouthed "police." I immediately did an about-face and headed back toward the elevator when a copper stepped around the far corner. I did the only thing I could; I turned and walked to my office.

Outside my door, Lieutenant Richard Powers, Jr. was waiting for me. I opened up and motioned him and the other cop inside. My uninvited guests sat down without my bidding.

"To what do I owe the honor, Lieutenant?" I asked unctuously.

Powers was a tough cop who made his way up the ranks through hard work and a very solid grasp of the law. If Powers pinched you, it was very unlikely you'd get off on any technicalities. Chances were the best you'd be able to do was strike a deal with the D.A. This was a good thing as far as I was concerned. We crossed paths a couple of times before and he always played it tough, but straight.

"You know Joe Marcus?" Right to the point, as expected.

"Uh-huh. He and his wife are good friends."

"He was a good friend," Powers said giving me a steely look.

"Was?" I asked innocently, nonchalantly putting my hands in my lap.

"Yeah, murdered. Somebody tipped us to where we could find his body early yesterday afternoon. You wouldn't know anything about that would you?"

"Why would you think that?" I parlayed.

"Because his wife said she hired you to find him."

"Uh-huh. She was worried, said he hadn't come home for a few days."

Powers gave the other cop a slant-wise look. "We also found your name and phone number on a piece of paper at the scene of the crime."

"You want to check my guns?" I inquired solicitously.

"Nope. I want to see your hands," he said flatly.

I swallowed hard and held them up.

He examined my knuckles and leaned forward with a nasty self-assured look on his face. "Marcus took quite a beating. Near as the doc can tell he died of a hematoma. Looks like you were on the other end of a beating like the one that killed him. You want to tell us your whereabouts yesterday?"

I fought for composure while my mind raced. None of my alternatives looked good. I was going to have to play things fast and loose and hope like hell. I told him about Gale, the missing money, and about Boots. I lied and said I fought with Boots' boys to account for my stitches and bruised knuckles. The odds were in my favor that he wouldn't waste his time checking my story with Doc Bax, Boots, or his men. He would probably check my phone calls and whereabouts though, so I leveled with him about Joe calling me. I told him Joe was already dead when I arrived at the house and how I immediately left to phone the precinct. When I finished, the other cop snorted and Powers gave him a look to remind him who was in charge.

"Pretty thin, Verriet."

"Yeah, but it's the truth."

"You believe the dame?"

"Gale?"

"Uh-huh."

"Up to a point. Everything fits except for Joe's killer. If Boots' men killed him, I figure Boots would have his money back by now. According to the word on the street, he's still searching."

"Makes sense. Keep going," he prodded.

Powers had something in mind, but he wasn't showing his hand. I decided I'd spilled enough. If Powers was going to run me in, he would have done so by now.

"That's it. But if I do find anything more, you'll be the first to know, Lieutenant."

His face tightened into a mask of controlled anger as he growled, "You make sure and do that, Verriet. And do it damn quick, because if you don't have anything for me soon, I'm sending the boys around to pick you up. I don't need the D.A. on my back."

He stood and motioned to his sidekick. They left and I reached in my bottom drawer for Old Granddad. I poured a couple inches of the amber nectar into a glass. I usually had lengthy conversations with pops, but events called for a very short discourse. I drowned my tonsils straight off before I refilled my glass. Drinking the chaser slowly, I tried to sort everything out. I had bought time with Powers, but not much. Mine was a short-lived pyrrhic victory at best.

Who killed Joe? Is Boots setting me up for Joe's murder? The time element is all wrong. No matter how I looked at the puzzle, Gale stuck out. *She fits in, but how?*

Although I didn't want to admit it, Teri was also a player in this game. She wasn't happy with her marriage. Maybe she found out Joe was having an affair with Gale. From what I had learned it was unlikely, but remained a possibility nevertheless. Regardless, Teri couldn't have killed Joe given the timing, and besides, Joe had taken one hell of a beating.

A woman might generate enough power with a blunt instrument, but it was unlikely a woman could haul him up the stairs unless he walked up under duress—say at gunpoint. And even then, it was extremely unlikely a woman could have knocked Joe out and tied him up without him putting up a fight. Unlike my hands, I remembered Joe's showed no evidence of having been in a fight. No, my money was on his killer being a man.

My thoughts switched to Powers. Junior could have easily hauled me in. He was an experienced cop who knew when to give his prime suspect enough rope either to stir things to a boil or to hang himself. Joe's killer relied on the latter when he had performed the Charleston on my knuckles. Sure, I had checked the house quickly; nevertheless, I was efficient enough to know there was no note with my phone number anywhere for the cops to find before I left. Either the killer, or someone else, came back and left that note after I had gone, or Powers lied about the note to spur me into action.

Then it hit me like a ton of bricks. The note Gale showed me that Joe supposedly left in the case when she first came to my office was similar to the one Powers' described. *Boots' henchmen had taken the note lying on my desk. Was it the same note?*

I'd have to remember to ask her about the note the next time we hooked up. Whether it was the same note or not, didn't prove anything. The only thing I knew for sure was that Powers' finding a note was a helluva coincidence, and in the detective business, one of the first lessons I had learned was that coincidences are as unlikely as a three-legged nag winning the Kentucky Derby.

Somebody was trying to frame me for Joe's murder. *Why? I'm only a minor player—a nobody who no one will miss—an expendable hardly worth the trouble. Someone is using me not for who I am but for what I am—someone with ties to Joe and a private detective. I'm a perfect fit amongst the hot seat candidates. So who are the other candidates? My two prime suspects for committing Joe's murder are Gale and Boots, and yet they're both my employers. Would they pay me just to set me up for Joe's murder? No one is that foolish. That leaves a plethora of other mobsters, and don't forget Teri.* This case was beginning to take on more twists than an octopus caught in a whirlpool.

One important question nagged at me. *How did Joe's killer find him just as I showed up on the scene?* As I said, coincidences rarely occur in my business and the killer's perfect timing stunk worse than week old potato peelings.

A small switch clicked on in my head and I somehow knew the answer—a leak. I glanced around my office. Tracing my phone's wires to the wall, I saw that someone had removed and replaced the wainscoting. I was slipping. I should have checked my telephone earlier. The Roy Olmstead case had recently been in all the papers telling how evidence against his bootlegging operation out west had been uncovered through wiretaps. My intruder must have installed the phone tap when he or she tore up my office.

Was the ransacking only a ruse to hide the real purpose for breaking in? The only party tied to the case with access to someone capable of setting the trap is Boots . . . or the cops. Powers might be giving me time in the hope of uncovering incriminating telephone conversations. With that unpleasant thought, I poured one more for the road.

Chapter Eleven

I fondly remembered Joe's former singer, Honey—a sultry blonde-haired gal who wore her tresses up on her head like the once ubiquitous Gibson girl. She had a knockout figure and a smoky contralto voice that made your corpora callosa stand at attention. I scanned the phone book until I found her address. She lived on the near West Side in a run-down area. I walked the block to the parking garage and retrieved my bucket of bolts. My flivver was as unreliable as a con's promise, and it wasn't very fast out of the blocks. I won't even mention what it was like to drive the heap when it rained, except to say I kept a large supply of towels handy in the compartment behind the seats. But with all her quirks, the little coupé was a blast to drive. A twenty-minute jaunt brought me to the front of an old two-story green clapboard house begging for paint and a roof job.

I half-expected the front door to fall off its hinges when I knocked. Nobody answered, and after another knock met with no response, I walked around and tried the back door. Unlocked, I walked in and immediately wished I hadn't. The stench was overpowering. I held my sleeve over my nose and made my way through the kitchen into the living room. In no time, the odor became unbearable and I had to beat a hasty retreat back outside where I gulped fresh air to clear my head. I took in as much oxygen as I could, held my breath and dashed back into the living room.

I found Honey in the main floor bedroom, sprawled out on a bed with her robe lying open—a bare breast exposed and her face a contorted frozen death mask. A quick examination of her once emaciated, now-bloated, body revealed nothing but ugly needle marks. My guess was she died of an overdose at least a week ago.

Back in my car, I sat and tried to remember how attractive and vibrant she looked when she first arrived on the scene singing for Mack Stout's band. I had trouble summoning her image from my memory banks as I kept seeing her in death's throes. Another talent lost to the world, another victim of a killer without a conscience. What a waste. Only someone who has experienced narcotic addiction can understand the flood of emotions I felt after finding her. You stand on the edge of the abyss knowing one wrong step will send you over without a shred of hope of ever coming back—and part of you yearns to go there.

I drove back to town with the window down in an attempt to rid my clothes of the stench. No matter how hard I breathed in the fresh air blowing in from Lake Michigan, I could still smell death.

I stopped off at Frankie's and asked him if I could use his phone. He placed a drink and phone in front of me and went down to the other end of the bar to give me privacy. I called Lieutenant Powers. When he answered, I told him about finding Honey.

"So you left a crime scene. I figured you for being brighter than that, shamus."

"Knock it off, Lieutenant. She's been dead for days, probably from an overdose. She was a former singer for Joe Marcus' band. Joe's wife told me Joe had to fire her due to her habit. If the doc finds out different let me know, will ya?"

"Oh sure. I got nothing better to do than keep some private snooper informed of my investigations. You sure there isn't some tie in to Marcus? Why did you go see her?"

"Just working all the angles."

"You think Marcus was killed because of a love triangle?"

"Who knows what a guy will do when some good-looking gal struts her stuff under his nose?" I replied thinking about Teri.

"Yeah," he agreed, "I've seen guys tumble who you'd never have thought it. Come up with something soon, Verriet. The D.A. was just here and the Captain is pushing. I'm going to have to feed you to the lions if you don't give me an alternative."

"Me! You sound like I'm your only suspect, Powers," I shouted in protest. "Am I the only one working on this case? What are you doing to earn the taxpayer's money, Junior?"

"You damn well know we're working on it, you son-of-a-bitch. I'd curb that smart mouth of yours if I were you and start working to pull your ass out of the fire, pal. You've got two days," he bellowed and slammed the receiver down in my ear.

Powers wasn't pulling any punches. He was serious about those two days. I looked in the back room and spotted Butters in his usual card game. When I caught his eye, I motioned with my head for him to join me and went back to the bar. Frankie pushed drinks in front of us as Butters hitched his tonnage up onto the stool next to me.

"Sorry to hear about Joe. Any idea who bumped him?"

"Just guesses. Lieutenant Powers wants to tag me for the job. He's using me as a tethered goat. He figures he can't lose. Either I bring him the killer, or he brings me in. Then again, maybe I'll get killed and he'll have more to go on to uncover the murderer. Nice, huh?"

I took a big gulp of beer. "I have the stinking suspicion he hopes it's the latter. Whoever did kill Joe beat him to death trying to find out where he hid whatever he took from Boots. The singer in Joe's band claims it was a bundle of cash. I hope to hell, Butters, you have something for me to help straighten out this mess."

"Not much new, pally. Only, Boots' numbers operation appears to be exactly like before he took things over from da other bosses."

"No changes at all?" I asked incredulously.

"Yeah, I've been thinkin' da same thing. Awful peculiar ain't it?"

I nodded in agreement.

"I asked around. He's kept everybody from McClanahan's old gang on his payroll—da runners, tallymen, even da two udder operators with all der boys. To top it off, he's increased all da guys' take, too. It's cockeyed! Sometin's not right. Everybody's makin' money and nobody is talkin'."

"Something's screwy all right. I never heard of a mobster taking over another's territory without a fight. Yet Boots keeps everybody on the payroll and pays them more. It doesn't figure."

Butters scratched his head for a minute. "Why keep everybody on the payroll? I think we hit on it before. Boots must be tryin' to sew up da numbers racket. He's makin' it into one big, smooth runnin' operation. Economy through numbers, no pun intended."

I reflected, "Yeah, but why in hell does Boots keep the other bosses and their boys around? He isn't stupid enough to think they'll be loyal. Maybe he's exercising the old axiom about keeping your friends close and your enemies closer."

"Ya gotta point, Nick, but if Boots took over my territory, I'd be gettin' ideas—like maybe I should grab da whole shebang. Wouldn't you?"

"Yeah, especially if I was looking to move up with one of the big bosses like Capone. Give me those guys' names and I'll see what I can find out. You work the runners and see what you can dig up, okay?"

"Sure, Nick," he said and extracted a small notepad from his pocket. He scribbled down the names, tore out the page and handed the paper to me.

"Let's back up a second, Butters. You said Boots killed McClanahan to start the whole numbers ball rolling, right?"

"Uh-huh."

"Do you think anybody in McClanahan's old outfit has a grudge against Boots for killing their boss?"

"Maybe, but like I told ya, Boots has put 'em all on easy street."

"Okay, so maybe I'm coming at this from the wrong angle. Do you think these other two operators he put the squeeze on have an axe to grind with Boots?" I asked scrutinizing the names he had jotted down.

"Could be. Maybe they're bidin' time, waitin' for da right moment to strike back. Like I said, I think da old bosses are playin' cat and mouse with Boots."

"Yeah, that's what I'm thinking, too. Be careful whom, and what, you ask, Butters. We may be sitting on a powder keg ready to explode any minute."

"Don't worry about me, I'm a big boy," he responded. "Oh, yeah, I checked on dat new dame, Storm. She worked at one of Vasco's joints in Detroit for about a year and dated one of da band members. Dat's where Boots discovered her. Nobody knows if der is, or was, anythin' between 'em. After he set up shop here in Chi, Boots brought her over."

"Thanks, Butters. Let's get together tomorrow about the same time and compare notes," I said and handed him a couple of ones.

The conversation with Butters put me further on edge. If there was a war looming between mob bosses, Butters and I were placing ourselves in the middle of the battlefield. I felt like a piece of chum dangling amongst hungry lake trout. I cursed Powers as I climbed in my chariot, goosed its kidneys, and pulled into traffic.

The first name on the paper belonged to Albert Hewitt—a minor operator who lived west of Canal Street in the warehouse district. His office was a small room that occupied the corner of a dark, grimy storage facility. Without knocking, I pried open a rusted metal door and waltzed into a dimly lit interior. Small dirty windows were set high on the walls. Dust motes danced in the shafts of light. I spotted a couple of goons playing cards on an overturned wooden crate.

"Al in?" I asked casually, "I've got a big bet for Saturday's game."

One of the guys looked up and pointed towards the back with his thumb. The bigger of the two intercepted me as I took my first step. He rasped, "Gotta check everybody first."

"No problem, palsy," I said agreeably since I had left my gun in the car. After a sloppy frisk, he waved me on and I moseyed through the arched doorway leading to the back. The old wood floorboards announced my presence with loud squeaks as I walked down a short hallway to the only door set in the wall to my right. I knocked once and a voice spoke, "Yeah, come on in."

Hewitt, small in frame with narrow rounded shoulders, had a long horse face with long dark brown hair hanging down the sides. The crown of his head was bald, dotted with dark brown splotches. He looked up at me through bloodshot rheumy eyes.

"What do you want?" he asked in a high-pitched squeal.

"I'd like to talk to you about your former business."

"Whaddya mean former. I'm here, ain't I?"

"Uh-huh, but you ain't the boss no more," I mimicked.

"Who the hell are you?"

"I'm just a guy who might be able to help you become boss again."

"Ain't interested. Beat it."

"What? You don't want to take over your old racket again? You'd rather work for Boots?"

"It's none of your damn business what I do. Now scram before I have the boys give you the bum's rush."

It was exactly as Butters had said. The operation was running as usual and Hewitt appeared unfazed by the new guard. There wasn't anything left to say, so I left.

The other name Butters had written on the piece of paper was Dave Dies, a self-appointed spokesperson for the coloreds living on the far South Side. I had never met him, but I knew about him. He was an outspoken radical according to the newspapers. Whenever a racial incident flared up in the city, they called upon Dies for a comment. He was Chicago University educated and highly articulate, but he spared no punches when it came to discussing the plight of the coloreds in the city. The newspapers didn't print most of what he said. Instead, they concentrated on misquotes and taking his words out of context to sell more copy.

Dies was in a completely different league from Boots. Unlike Boots, Dies kept the numbers running on the South Side to benefit the community at large. He carved a comfortable living for himself, but he used the lion's share of the money his various operations yielded to build playgrounds and a youth club in a neighborhood that no one north of the racial divide gave two hoots about.

Knowing what I did about Dies made it highly unlikely Boots could have wrested control of the numbers from him. On the other hand, Butters was never cavalier with his information. When he said Boots had taken over Dies' numbers, I knew I could bank on it. If Boots had sewn up all the numbers business between Hewitt's and Dies' territories, he was taking in quite a haul.

I stopped on the way for a quick sandwich and beer at an old neighborhood bar. When I jumped back behind the wheel of my chariot and steered into traffic, I noticed a black Dodge pulling out from the curb a half block down the street. I made a couple of right hand turns followed by a quick left and my pursuer did the same. The bozo following me pulled his hat down so I couldn't obtain a good look at his face. After another fifteen minutes of playing cat and mouse, I lost him at a busy intersection and breathed a sigh of relief. Two white guys in an all-colored neighborhood could spell trouble. As it was, I already felt as conspicuous as a first-time attendee in a nudist colony.

Dies' operated right out in the open, a neat brick building next to a neighborhood grocery. He obviously provided kickbacks to the local constabularies. A sign depicting a silhouetted pair of black dice sporting yellow pips against a white background was pasted on the picture window in the lower right. Torchies was painted in gilt lettering in the middle of the window.

Three guys wearing black suits, colorful shirts and ties, black felt derbys, and black patent leather oxfords were hanging around out front. They made no attempt to hide the gats tucked into their waistbands.

I felt naked as I climbed out of my car and more than a little nervous. They stopped their conversation and glared at me as I approached.

"What do you want, white boy?" one of them asked pugnaciously, placing his mitt on the handle of his roscoe.

"I'd like to talk to Mr. Dies," I said plainly. "Tell him, it's Nick Verriet."

"What's your business?" one of the others challenged in a hoarse voice. He had visible scar tissue around both eyes and a broad flat nose set at an angle—probably a former boxer who had taken too many shots to his voice box. I carefully reached into my pocket, withdrew a business card and handed it to him.

"Tell him I'd like to see him be the boss again."

Flat nose gave me a hard look before he went inside without looking at my card. His two cohorts stood guard duty, both of their guns drawn and pointed at my midsection. The seconds passed like hours as I stood immobile sweating profusely. Flat nose returned in a few moments and nodded to the lad on my left who stood poised like a tiger that hadn't been fed in a week. His hands did a quick frisk before he motioned to me to follow him through the door.

Inside, he swung part of a countertop up and we passed through the opening and continued down a hall to a wood-paneled office where a guy wearing a loose fit, double-breasted suit with a white shirt and striped bow tie sat behind a steel and wood art-deco desk. He ordered my escort to shut the door and motioned for me to sit down.

"Verriet. You the guy who found Newt's killer?" he asked in a deep baritone.

"Yeah." Newt had been a jazz musician for a local South Side band until he was discovered hanging from a railroad trestle.

He nodded. "Not many white guys would have worked so hard to find a colored's killer in this town."

"I was getting paid for it," I said matter-of-factly.

He nodded again and said, "Yeah, but most white guys wouldn't have taken the job, even for pay. So what's this shit, you wanting me to be the boss?"

"Heard you're workin' for Boots now and wondered how you liked it. Maybe you'd like things to go back being the way they were before Boots hit town."

"Who the hell told you that?" he asked as his eyes narrowed.

"Nobody told me. It just adds up."

"Somebody paying you to add it up?"

"Nope."

"Then why you so interested?"

I decided to make a play I hoped wouldn't backfire. "Joe Marcus was a good friend of mine. I'm convinced he was killed because he became involved in something to do with Boots. I'm trying to find Joe's killer. If I find out Boots had anything to do with it, he won't be the boss of anyone anymore."

He sat and studied me for a couple of minutes in silence. His soft brown eyes looked far away, and he said, "I was sorry to read about Marcus. A good man . . . one of the few of you whites worth a shit. Never made no difference to him what color of skin a man had, long as he could swing. I hope you find his killer, but I don't see how that's my business."

"Not even if I can prove Boots was behind it?"

"Nope. Things would just go back to the way they were before."

"So you don't mind working for Boots now?"

He nonchalantly shrugged his shoulders. "I make my money either way."

"Thanks for your time, Mr. Dies."

As I opened the door, he said, "You took a hell of a chance, Verriet, coming here like you did. This conversation is going to stay between the two of us, but I'd be looking over my shoulder if I was you."

Chapter Twelve

I took my time driving back downtown and thought over what Dies had said. *Was he warning me to keep out of the middle because he is going to move in on Boots? Or does he think one of the other bosses is poised for action?* The casual way he dismissed Boots made me think he was marshaling his forces against Boots—biding his time until the situation was ripe. I hoped to hell I was watching from the sidelines when those two clashed.

Dusk was giving way to a warm humid evening as I made a quick stop at my office to check for messages. There weren't any, so I jumped back in my heap and drove over to Roscoe's. The hatcheck girl was a blonde dish, tall with good curves and a winning smile. She looked bored, and with good reason from the looks of the empty room behind her. I suspected she was more window dressing than anything else.

"The big boss in?" I asked her.

She frowned before she replied, "Yeah, but I wouldn't be too eager to talk to him. He's been a real bear lately."

"Maybe you should try a little honey," I suggested.

"Nah, he ain't my type, but with you I might try a bit of sugar."

"What time do you get off tonight, sweet stuff?"

"Two."

"Maybe I'll see you then. I'm Nick by the way."

"April. If not tonight, I'm here every night but Tuesday."

"I'll remember, sugar," gave her a wink, and walked down the hall.

Sam stood waiting ever vigilant. He opened the office door before I had a chance to knock and followed me inside. A tense atmosphere permeated the office.

Boots gave me a hard look when I eased my chassis into a chair. He turned, grabbed a cigar out of a small humidor sitting atop a side bureau behind his desk, carefully snipped off the end, and swiveled his chair to face me. He held a lighter to his stogie and stared at me over the flame. "I hear you've been a busy man, Verriet."

I shrugged in reply.

"I asked you to locate my materials and I find out you're sticking your nose into my business where it doesn't belong."

"I have to check out all the possibilities, don't I?"

He took a couple puffs on his cigar, gave me a hard stare, and poked it at me. "Stay away from my business associates. Stick to finding out who killed Joe and find my case, understand?"

"Uh-huh." Either Hewitt or Dies had talked to him. My money was on Hewitt. A slapping sound echoed in the room. Sam, honing a straight edge razor on a strop held between his foot and left hand, was making quite a show of his prowess with his ugly weapon of choice. I fought to calm my nerves by focusing on Boots.

"The way I figure, somebody close to you knew what Joe took—somebody involved in your business. How the hell can I find out who it is without getting involved in your business?"

"You're wrong, Verriet. Nobody connected to my business is involved. Somebody on the outside killed Joe, somebody he knew. If it was anybody in my organization, I'd have already found out about it by now." Boots snarled.

"How can you be so sure?"

"Listen, smart guy, it's not open for debate. Take my word and start looking elsewhere, otherwise . . ." he ended with a knowing look to Sam the Barber.

He let the rest go as an open threat, so I switched the subject. "Have you had your boys tailing me?"

"Nope," he said with prosaic abruptness.

"I've had at least two tails."

Boots frowned and gave Sam a quick look. "You better be careful, Verriet. I wouldn't like it if you found my goods and somebody took them away from you. I hold you responsible, got that? If anybody else gets my goods, it's your neck, understand?" Sam emphasized Boots' statement with another loud slap of the strop.

"Yeah, Boots, you're coming across loud and clear." *Great. Powers on one end, Boots on the other, both putting the squeeze on.* I stood up, leaned over his desk and said, "Now I'll give you a piece of advice. If I was you, I'd check on my business associates one more time because I figure the odds are better than even money somebody in your own organization is responsible for Joe's death," I said with a sneer and walked out before he had a chance to reply.

Bobby met me at the hallway entrance. "Nick, I thought I spotted you. Man, can you help me? I'm barely holding the band together."

"What can I do?"

"Fill in for the bass player—play guitar. I need some rhythm."

"You call that help, Bobby? I haven't played with a band in a long time."

"Yeah, but you keep in shape playing when you arrange don't you?"

"Somewhat," I agreed hesitantly.

"Just tonight. For me and the band, huh?"

"All right, but don't say I didn't warn you," I replied reluctantly.

He grinned, grabbed my arm, led me to the rear of the bandstand and pointed to an old beat up guitar. It was a Gibson L5 like the one I owned, except you'd hardly recognize it from all the knocks this one had taken over the years.

While I warmed up, Bobby brought out a handful of music— the numbers for the night, and placed them in front of me. The guitar sounded off-key when I began to play through the numbers. I experimented with different chord changes and made notes in the margins to remind me of the tricky parts. I barely finished before the rest of the band joined me. As we began to play the first number, I waved my hand to Bobby and he gave a cut signal to the band.

"What's wrong, Nick."

"Bobby, this guitar's neck is so warped, I can't keep it in tune. I have an idea. Give me a middle 'C'."

When he blew the note, I listened with my eyes closed and played the note on the second, fourth, and six strings, "Yeah, there's nearly a half step difference. You need rhythm, so what if I tune the low strings for rhythm and I'll tune up the high strings for short breaks? I won't play them together, but I'll emphasize the heck out of the bass."

"Sounds good to me, Nick. Whatever you can do to kick the rhythm—anything's better than what we've been doing lately. Let's try a couple numbers and see," he said hopefully.

I was sweating by the time we finished with the second number. The stress was getting to me. Playing would have been a real chore even if I didn't have to account for the poor shape of the guitar. When the boys hit the fast numbers, I concentrated like mad. It was all I could do to keep up with the pace.

"That wasn't too bad," Bobby said when we stopped.

"Yeah, but it wasn't too good either. Do you still want me?"

"You betcha, Nick," he said to my dismay.

"All right, let me practice until it's time to go on. And get me a couple of drinks before I change my mind."

Bobby grinned at me and walked over to the bar. I played non-stop for the next hour and felt a little bit better by the time I finished practicing. *I just might pull this clambake off.*

I grabbed another drink from the bar while the other band members loosened up on stage. We kicked off with *Stardust* and I settled into the groove. I relaxed and even began to enjoy myself with a couple of tunes and drinks under my belt. I had forgotten how much I missed playing in a band. Gale joined us and I had to admit she was a damn good canary. The joint was almost full by the time we finished the first set.

During the second set, somebody made a special request and I accompanied Gale. At break, she came up to me and enthused, "That was great, Nick. You never told me you could play."

"It never came up."

"You know something, I think I like singing to your accompaniment better than with the band."

"Makes sense—a simple guitar accompaniment highlights your talent better."

"Do you really think so, Nick?"

"No doubt about it."

"How about you and me working on a more intimate atmosphere after the last set?" she asked with smoldering eyes.

"Sure," I agreed and felt my face flush.

We played for another two hours. Gale sang even better than before. She immersed herself into the spirit of the music and the crowd reacted appreciably. I couldn't help notice that Chuck was staring daggers at me as we wrapped up the last set and the band members began to pack up their instruments.

Gale grabbed my arm in hers. "You ready to blow this joint?"

"Your place or mine?"

"Yours if you've got something to drink. I'm all out."

After I finished tidying up the music scattered about, I settled my bar tab and motioned to Gale that I was ready to leave.

She laughed when she saw my struggle buggy. "What is this, a model T?"

"It's a Mitchell. She's not much to look at on the outside, but she's got some pep and is built better than anything Ford has on the market. Gale swung her shapely gams in as I jumped behind the wheel and stomped my brogan down on the starter. I kicked the car in gear and drove off. The air was sultry, wrapping me in a blanket of anticipation as only nighttime can. A perfect evening, I suggested we take a drive up north and come back into the city on Lake Shore Drive to enjoy the bright stars and city lights. Driving into the city from the north was one of my favorite things to do on such a night and Gale must have liked it, too, because she was quiet, absorbing the magnificent view.

When we reached my apartment, she said, "We make a great duo, Nick." Her exclamation made me think about the vicissitudes of women. We were good together, but not as good as she made us out to be.

"Not bad for a first go," I admitted.

I fixed us a couple of highballs and handed her one as she studied the sheet music on my drafting table.

"You've all kinds of hidden talents, don't you?" she chided.

"Yes ma'am," I obliged.

She came over to me, set her drink down, and asked salaciously, "I know you're good at music. I wonder what else you're good at."

I pulled her to me and we kissed until she broke the embrace, her eyes ablaze and chest heaving. She reached around her dress and unhooked the top latch before she deftly unzipped the back, letting her silken garment and slip fall to the floor in folds. She stepped out of the dress, stood there in lace bra and panties and gave me a full-frontal exhibition. She came back into my arms and we kissed again, this time with an animal ferocity that consumed us.

The first time we made love was on my sofa—primal, quick and selfish in our demands. The second time was in my bedroom and we took our time, exploring each other. Mutually exhausted, we both fell asleep.

A light sleeper since the war, I felt her move from against me sometime during the night. She slipped out of bed and crept noiselessly out of the room. When she didn't return after a few minutes, I quietly went looking for her. I peeked around the corner into my living room. Bent over in front of my bookshelf, she was methodically pulling out each book and checking the inside for a hidden compartment and the space the book had occupied before sliding each volume back into place. I returned to the bedroom. *What the hell! Let her look all she wants,* I thought and went back to sleep.

Chapter Thirteen

Friday

Gale was gone when I awoke again. *Did she sleep with me just to search my apartment?* The thought bothered me—bruised my male ego, but I'd live. I had motives of my own. With a shrug, I crawled out of bed and shuffled across the hall to the kitchen. I spooned coffee into the basket, and placed the works into the pot. My percolator began its ritual gurgling a few moments after I fired up the burner. Following a shave and shower, I sat and ate some stale strudel washed down with a couple cups of java. I took the last cup of coffee to the living room, plopped down onto my beat-up sofa and set my cogitative wheels into motion.

Was Joe killed by the guy who I spotted walking toward the house when I arrived? The dog's barking supported this notion. Whoever the assailant was, he beat Joe up to find out something—or money, according to Gale. Did Joe tell? If he did, neither Boots nor Gale knew about it because they were still looking for it, whatever 'it' was.

Boots and Gale—what's between those two? Boots brings her in from Detroit, yet she doesn't claim any allegiance to him. Is the whole thing an act and she's really his ally? It's a definite possibility based upon their shared past. If she's working with Boots, then the scene in my office with his thugs was all a set-up. But why me? Why embroil me in their machinations? It didn't make sense Boots would risk exposing his operation to somebody from the outside. He proved that when he found out I had talked to Al Hewitt and Dave Dies. He told me in no uncertain terms to stay out of his business.

Then there was Teri. *She said she wanted to leave Joe, but now I wasn't so sure she meant it. She was taking Joe's death very hard. Could she be the joker in the deck and really be in with Boots? Is she putting on an act for my benefit? Look how much I never knew about Joe. How much did she and Joe change after they were married?*

Now that we had experienced a brief reunion, I knew I had never fallen out of love with Teri. She was a brand burnt onto my soul, my very being. Sure, I had a respite with Gale last night, but it meant nothing to me. Gale satisfied my physical needs, nothing more than a surrogate for Teri. *Or was she?*

"Shit, shit, shit," I muttered under my breath. If I wasn't involved in this case, Teri and I would be moving forward with our lives—together. But I *was* involved. And Lieutenant Powers was making sure I stayed involved. What a mess.

I reasoned the key lay somewhere with Boots and his organization. I decided to visit O'Malley, the former owner of Roscoe's. Maybe he could provide an answer or two, but first, I'd go see Teri, see how she was doing. I hoped by now she was over her initial shock of Joe's death.

The door opened before I knocked, and Teri explained, "Saw you pull up, Nick."

We sat at the kitchen table across from each other. "How you doing, kiddo?" I asked cheerfully, but I needn't have bothered. She had dark circles under her eyes and appeared to have slept in her clothes. One look at her dashed all my hopes.

"I'm okay, I guess," she replied weakly.

"Anything I can do for you?"

She looked up at me sorrowfully and replied, "I just need some time, Nick."

"Sure, I understand. I know I haven't said this in a long time, Teri, but I need you to know that I love you. I don't think I've ever stopped loving you over the years."

Tears welled up in her eyes, and she brushed at them with the back of her hand. "Nick, I know you mean well, but now's not the time," she sniffled. "I need time to sort everything out."

"Sure, honey. I was thinking of running up to the cabin again and looking around some more. Want to go with?"

She silently shook her head 'no.'

"All right. Remember, I'm only a phone call away. You need anything, anything at all, call me. No matter what, call me," I repeated like a broken record.

"Thanks," she replied softly.

I stood up, walked to the front door, and quietly shut the screen door behind me. My stomach felt like somebody had taken a jackhammer to it. My whole world was crumbling around me. As I drove back downtown, I started to get steamed.

Why in the hell did this have to happen? I renewed hope only to see the relationship I yearned for fall apart again. I raged against the powerlessness that engulfed me and yelled a string of invectives at the top of my lungs. *The only thing that might work is to solve Joe's murder and hope time will straighten everything out between us.* With that strategy in mind, a glimmer of hope seeped back into my world again. Hope—the cruelest four-letter word in the English language.

Chapter Fourteen

The fuse I had lit in anger set off an internal inferno by the time I reached Jim O'Malley's house on Belmont. Somebody was going to pay and pay dearly once I laid my hands on Joe's killer. It was all I could do to be civil when O'Malley ushered me into his living room. The place was warm and inviting and he motioned me to sit in one of two lounge chairs facing a fumed-oak Victrola.

I introduced myself, but I needn't have since he remembered me as one of his semi-regular customers. O'Malley had thick gray hair and bushy black eyebrows set over black eyes that always seemed to shine of wisdom. One of the lucky people blessed with charm, his rosy-red face lit up whenever he smiled. He always made you feel good for some ineffable reason.

"Nick, long time, no see. To what do I owe the honor?"

His jovial manner temporarily erased all vestiges of my ill humor. "As usual, I'm on a case, and it involves Boots. I'm hoping you might be able to fill in a few of the blanks."

"I'm not sure I have much to offer on that account, but I'll help if I can," he affirmed.

"What can you tell me about Boots buying your place? I thought they'd have to carry you out of there before you'd quit."

He nodded sagely and replied, "You and me both, laddie. That man is daft, you know that? He paid me over three times what I would have asked for the place if I had put it on the market. Saints be praised, how could I refuse, I ask you now? Especially since those hypocritical sons in Washington passed the Volstead Act."

"I see your point. Why would he pay so much? The place can't be making a whole lot more since he changed the scenery, can it?"

"Funny, it's the very question I've been asking meself. Makes no sense, now does it? Even if he doubles the trade, it'll take him a blessed seven, eight years to break even."

"That's applesauce," I agreed. "Boots isn't stupid. What could he possibly do to make the investment worthwhile?" I wondered aloud.

"I wish to heaven I knew. Whatever he's about can't be legal," he stated.

"Yeah, I think you hit the nail on the head, Jim. So what's next for you?"

"I'm thinking of a nice long vacation to Ireland. Might move there. I can buy a good piece of property near the Strand. Maybe even meet a fetching Irish lass and raise a family," he said with a mischievous wink.

When I thanked him for his time, he said wistfully, "I miss the old place, Nick. Running a pub gets in your blood."

"Maybe you can open one in Ireland."

"Ah, now there's a thought lad," he said with a wistful smile.

"Whatever happens, I wish you luck."

"You, too. Stop by when you've more time," he said. We shook hands and I left thinking how nothing good lasts for long. It was highly unlikely we'd ever meet again. Time is an evil landlord; it takes away the good and leaves only hope and despair in its wake. Someday, somebody ought to do something about it.

Chapter Fifteen

I squeezed my flivver's gizzard and headed north. About ten miles from the Wisconsin border, a glance in the review mirror revealed I had a tail again. Immersed deep in thought for most of the drive, I had no idea how long he had been there. He could have been tailing me all day since I was too preoccupied with my plight to take sensible precautions. I was slipping—something I couldn't afford to do or I'd be pushing up daisies in no time flat.

I took my foot off the gas after taking a big sweeping curve. My shadow came up close enough for me to get a good look at the car—a black Dodge with a lot more horsepower than I could kick out of my chariot. If I were in the city, I would stand a chance at losing him, but not here on the open road.

I kept my speed steady and eased back in the seat. My tail diligently stayed an even distance from me. I approached the turn-off for the county road and considered my alternatives to lose him before I reached Joe's cabin. I didn't have long to work out a strategy—my cogitative wheels barely made another revolution before he closed the distance between us.

Up ahead was another curve set on a rise with an embankment that sloped down into a stand of tall pines. My tail picked up more speed until he was only a dozen car lengths behind me. If this was the same tail Teri and I had on our earlier trip to the cabin, he was making sure I wasn't going to shake him at the last turn by Joe's. *This lad has something more malicious in mind than a simple tail job.*

I pressed the accelerator to the floor to little effect. Horsepower wasn't one of my rust bucket's better qualities. Begrudgingly, my buggy accelerated until she began to rattle so bad it was all I could do to keep her pointed straight. As the Dodge bore down on me, I turned to get a good look at my pursuer. He had a head of dark hair and an intense look on a gaunt face that struck me as vaguely familiar.

It was useless to try to outrun him. I waited until he was two car lengths away, then I tugged on the wheel, switched lanes and stomped on the brakes. His car's tires squealed in protest. Volumes of smoke discharged from his wheel wells as he threw out all four anchors and veered around me. Instead of plummeting down the embankment, he jerked to a stop about a hundred feet in front of me, jumped out of his car with gat drawn, and let loose two rounds. Kachow! Kachow! The first bullet splintered my windshield on the passenger side, and the second tore a hole in the passenger seat.

My perambulator stalled with my sudden stop. My assailant ran towards me, firing at random. I stomped on the starter and hoped like hell the engine would turn over. My chariot's engine protested and I cursed her birth. With a loud backfire, she sprang to life. I slammed the gearshift in reverse and mashed my foot on the gas. I heard four more shots resound over the whine of my buggy's straining engine as I wound a serpentine trail backwards. When I was a safe distance away, I stopped and watched my attacker turn and run back towards his car.

I hit the gas and peeled after him, but my betsy hadn't the gumption to catch him before he reached the safety of his vehicle. He backed across the road in an effort to block both lanes and prevent me from going around him. I swung the wheel hard to the right hoping to pass on the shoulder, but my rust bucket was too shaky. The tires broke loose when they hit the gravel skirting and my flivver went into a vicious skid. The back end swung around heading for the embankment.

I had little hope of survival if my barge didn't hold ground. Desperately, I grasped the wheel with sweaty hands, jerked hard in the opposite direction, but the car had a mind of its own. Swerving close to the edge, my back tires suddenly hit a fallen tree branch which caused the rear-end to buck up with a violent lurch. I frantically grabbed the wheel to keep from hitting the windshield or being thrown out of the car. The momentum crazily swung the front around until the rear tires gained traction once more.

My tin-betsy reached the edge of the embankment, pivoted, and the back tires went over the edge, racing backwards down the embankment. A quick glance over my shoulder revealed the tree line only fifty feet away. I yanked the gearshift and smashed both feet on the brake, nearly pushing the pedal through the floor. My bucket gradually slowed until the bumper clipped first one tree, then another, and came to rest.

I pried my shaking hands off the wheel and stared up the hill. I sat and carefully watched along the ridgeline until my nerves steadied. After ten minutes transpired with still no sign of my tail, I climbed out of my car and did a damage assessment. Cracked windshield and numerous dents were visible. On hands and knees, I inspected the undercarriage. Everything appeared intact, but I wouldn't know the extent of damage, especially to the suspension and drivetrain, until she was back on the road.

Keeping a steady watchful eye, I slowly climbed the embankment. The Dodge was nowhere in sight as I huffed the last few feet to the road apron. Fifteen minutes later a car approached. I waved my arms in distress, but the driver, a middle-aged woman, hit the gas and sped away. I realized the same result with the next two buggies. If I was a woman, a flashed gam at the next man would surely elicit help. My legs weren't bad, but I doubted anybody would stop for a closer look.

Eventually, a carload of young guys pulled over, and after I explained my predicament, they took up my cause as a manly challenge to extradite my car from its tree-lined labyrinth. Two guys planted themselves behind the rear bumper while the other two guys each grabbed a door handle. I climbed in, started the engine and gave them a shout. The car gained traction and to my astonishment made tracks up the steep embankment until we safely reached the top. The guys even helped me change the flat tire my buggy had picked up from hitting one of the trees. I expressed my gratitude by handing their driver ten clams to divvy amongst them.

Before continuing my sojourn, I walked to where the shooter had been. The shiny brass shell casings were easy to spot in the bright sunshine. Gingerly, I picked them up and stuck them in my suit pocket. Plopping myself down behind the steering wheel, I started out again, but this time I kept a lookout and slowed down as I approached blind curves. My attacker didn't show for a rematch.

Another set of car tracks were visible in the grass next to Joe's cabin when I finally arrived. I didn't knock because the back door swung loosely open. I peered in a side window as I walked toward the lakeside of the cabin. Nothing stirred inside, but to be safe I entered through the screened-in porch. Everything was a shambles.

The old couch's fabric was slashed, the stuffing ripped out. The kitchen cabinets' contents lay strewn about the floor in the small living space. The door was open on the little wood burning stove, and the stove's pipe ripped off from its base up to the ceiling. Even the floorboards lay pried up at random intervals. Whoever searched the place left nothing unscathed.

The violence wrought upon the cabin, resting tranquilly in north woods' innocence, angered me, as if something vile had raped nature herself. I let out a string of invectives and searched through the cans and bottles in the kitchenette until I found an unopened bottle of whiskey. I cracked the seal. One snozzle told me it was the good stuff from Canada, and I poured a half glass full. Out on the porch, I settled into an old wood rocking chair, sipped my drink, and stared out at the glimmering sky-blue lake water.

The natural serenity of the setting, coupled with the sun, alcohol, and nervous exhaustion soon put me to sleep. I awoke to a screeching sound, an osprey rejoicing over a fish held in its talons. In another hour, the sun would set behind the tall pines bordering the property. The quietude provided a stark contrast to city life. *Maybe I should move up here. And do what?* I asked myself sorrowfully.

I tidied up, stomped floorboards back into place, and fixed the stovepipe as best I could before leaving. During the drive home, I tried to concentrate on the case particulars, but my mind was preoccupied by the thought tomorrow was Saturday which marked the expiration of my two days allowance by Lieutenant Powers.

I was bushed by the time I pulled into the underground parking garage of my apartment building. The elevator took me up to my apartment where I made myself a quick drink and settled onto my sofa. I mulled over the day's events. The guy who tried to kill me had looked familiar, but I couldn't place him. I definitely hadn't seen him around Boots' place. *Was the joker trying to kill me to whittle down the competition in the mad race to find the loot? Did someone hire him? If so, who? Whoever he was, he wanted to find Boots' materials. Why else ransack Joe's cabin? And how in hell did he know about the cabin?*

They were all fair questions that I added to my long list of unanswered puzzle pieces. Something tugged at my subconscious, a nagging notion the missing puzzle piece lay just beyond my grasp. There is always a key piece to every puzzle which demands two essential applications—its identification and its use. *What was I missing and how did the missing link tie in?*

I finished my drink and made another. Fetching pen and paper, I sat down and made a list of what I considered the pertinent points of the case. When the list was finished, I rearranged the items according to different scenarios. Each time I tried a different combination something appeared askew—not as a glaring problem with my logic—more a mismatch with my gut instinct. I kept at the exercise until I nodded off.

Chapter Sixteen

Saturday

When I looked at my wristwatch, it was nine o'clock in the morning. I picked up my notes where they lay on the floor and shuffled into the bedroom where I stripped off my clothes, scraped my face, and climbed into the shower. Afterwards, I donned a striped gray three-button suit with a white-collar dress shirt, and a pair of black and white oxfords.

After a breakfast of scrambled eggs, toast, orange juice, and coffee, I settled back and read the weekend paper. A big article about Germany's on-going political struggles was on the front page. "What a waste of lives," I muttered and thought about the guys from my old platoon, many of whom never returned home. *Wasn't the World War supposed to be the war to end all wars? What a joke! What did we Americans go overseas and fight for when only a few years later the politics in Europe are heating up all over again?*

I mulled over how naïve and disillusioned I had been. The only reason I succumbed to the draft was the fact I was too ignorant to consider my alternatives and the machinations underlying the war. I wondered what my German father would say now if he lived to read this newspaper article. After he married my mother, who was French, they left Europe for a better life in this country.

My parents did quite well in their adopted home. Too bad they didn't live longer to enjoy their success. On the other hand, they didn't see the shambles I had become after one of my platoon members stepped on a land mine that filled me with enough shrapnel to add a pound to my weight. "Qu'ils reposent en paix," I said softly, crunching the page into a ball, and tossing it into the waste can.

I filled a glass of tap water, sat down at my small kitchen table, and studied my notes from last night. Try as I might, no new insights were forthcoming. I decided it was time to check and see if Butters had uncovered anything for me. I shoved my .45 into my holster, and rode the elevator down to the basement. My parking spot was towards the far end of the massive garage. Plumbing pipes and conduit lines for the apartment building lined the cement ceiling. I ducked my six-foot plus chassis under the largest of the pipes running the length of the garage.

The movement saved my life. A dull thud sounded beside me, immediately followed by a sharp gun report that echoed off the cement walls. In two shakes, I jumped behind the nearest car and scuttled toward the rear bumper pinned against the wall. Silence followed. I scrunched over and peered under the car. Looking around I didn't see anyone's brogans. I drew out my heater and grasped it with both hands. Methodically, I placed one foot in front of the other while I stayed hunched over and waddled around the car.

I had no idea from which direction the shot had come. My only recourse was to shuffle along, away from my flivver, take a periodic look underneath the parked cars and hope to catch sight of the shooter or wait for a diversion. Squatting soon had my quadriceps screaming for relief.

I had traversed about fifty feet when I accidently clipped the side of a Plymouth with my gun. A sharp ping sounded and I hurriedly hauled my carcass to the opposite end of the car and stole a glimmer to see if the gunner was visible. My assailant ripped off another blast and I felt a tug on my left side, but this time I placed the shooter on my left. Turning, I crouched and lamped a figure who ducked down and withdrew behind a cream-colored sedan.

My side began to sting and my shirt was blood soaked. Blood trailed to my britches waistline and I began to feel a warm trickle run down my leg. Suddenly, the elevator opened and a young couple walked out talking cheerfully. The guy carried a beach bag and the woman a picnic basket. I had a choice to make, either go after my pursuer or take advantage of the couple's presence to make it back to the elevator safely. Hurried footsteps sounded. I took a quick peek around the car's bumper and spotted the shooter running to beat hell toward the exit at the far end of the garage.

I wanted to take a shot at him, but there was the couple to consider, and at this distance, I'd have little chance of hitting him. I felt a bit woozy when I stood up and reached out an arm to the nearest car to steady myself. I took a few deep breaths and steered my carriage toward the elevator. The couple stopped in their tracks and stared at me in silence as I walked toward them.

"Good morning," I said with a forced smile.

The guy grasped the woman's arm and rushed her to the side of the garage away from me. I couldn't blame him. My suit pants were dirty from playing hide and seek with the shooter, my shirt was bloody, and I had momentarily forgotten about the gun clutched tightly in my right hand.

Back in my apartment, I stripped off my suit coat and shirt to examine the wound in the bathroom mirror. The bullet had grazed a shallow four-inch furrow along one of my short ribs. After cleaning the wound and taping half a dozen gauze bandages over it, I donned a clean shirt and pants. I stuffed all my dirty clothes into an old army bag, lugged it back to the garage and tossed it into the passenger seat of my car.

I grabbed a flashlight from under the seat and walked to where the shooter had been stationed. A quick search revealed two bullet casings, both from a .38, not absolute proof the shooter was the same person driving the Dodge, but it looked that way. I was at the top of some torpedo's bumpery list. If I kept stirring the pot, I'd either flush him out or I'd fill the remaining plot in the family gravesite. With that pleasant thought, I drove over to Doc Bax's office.

Bax worked an abbreviated schedule on Saturdays. Sandy ignored the outraged looks from the patients in the waiting room and quickly hustled me into an examination room when I told her sotto voce that I'd been shot. I only had time to take off my shirt and hang it on the hook at the back of the door before Maria entered.

She took one look at my side, which had turned a bright red around the edges of my makeshift bandage, shook her head back and forth. "The doctor should charge you rent. What happened this time?"

"Somebody shot me."

"You mean with a gun?" she asked awe-stricken.

"Yeah, is there another way?"

"Why did somebody shoot you?"

"I dunno. Maybe they didn't like my aftershave."

She peeled off the tape and gently removed the gauze bandages to reveal an ugly red gash, caked with dried blood. As soon as she pulled the last gauze pad off, the wound began to bleed again.

"Hurry and give me something to absorb the blood, Maria," I said cupping my hand against my side, "before it reaches my pants. I'm down to my last clean pair," I exclaimed.

She tossed me a large gauze pad, and said, "That ought to do. I'll give you more after I clean the wound. Does it hurt?"

"It burned at first, now it stings and aches."

"I always wondered what it would be like to be shot. You're the only gunshot victim I can remember treating," she declared.

"Do I get a plaque on the wall or something?"

"No, only some more shots," she said a bit too enthusiastically for my money as she whipped out a hypodermic, stabbed the end through the rubber top of a small vial, turned it upside down and pulled out the plunger to fill the needle.

"Sit on the examination table," she ordered. "I'm going to numb the area and cleanse the wound before the doctor examines you." Without hesitating, she jabbed me with the needle around the periphery of the gash.

"I'll tell the doctor you're here," she said after she emptied the needle's contents into my side and temporarily covered me up.

In a few minutes, she returned with Doc Bax in tow. He took one look at my wound and said, "You're a lucky man, Nick. A few inches left and you would have been killed. I take back my earlier assessment of our respective occupations. Why did someone shoot you?"

"This sounds crazy, Doc, but I don't know. The case I'm working on has more angles than a Chinese puzzle box."

"I should report this to the police, you know."

"Hell yes," I replied. "Call it in to Lieutenant Powers in homicide, he's ready to lock me up anyway," I said breezily. "I'll even give you his number before I leave. Let me skedaddle before you do, though."

"Only for you, Nick. Maria will finish with you. Try to rest quietly for a couple of days and change the dressing every twelve hours. You should be fine in a week or so. Come back Tuesday and I'll take another look. I'll remove your stitches then, too," he said after he checked out my scalp.

"Thanks, doc," I said as he jotted a few quick notes on a form and stuck it in a folder.

Maria returned and gave me another shot before she taped some gauze over my wound. She handed me a paper bag containing extra bandages, tape, and a tube of some gunk to apply to my side. I jotted Powers' name and number on a piece of paper, handed it to her, and said, "Give this to the Doc. He'll know what it's about. And thanks for the quick attention, Maria. I'll remember you at Christmas time."

"You better give me my present now, Nick. I doubt you'll see Christmas at the rate you're going."

Chapter Seventeen

After I left the doctor's office, I felt tighter than an overwound clock spring. The cumulative effects of two attempts on my life, coupled with my feelings for Teri, had me on edge, both physically and mentally.

My time was up with Powers. He was sure to have me hauled in after Doc Bax called in the shooting. I decided to stay away from my apartment and office as I climbed into my buggy and sat staring at nothing. The awful truth was, I didn't know what to do next. *Some P.I.* All I could think of doing was to keep stirring things up until they came to a boil. With a shrug, I decided to retrace my steps beginning with the house where Joe was killed. Maybe I had missed something earlier that would set me on the killer's track.

Kids were playing baseball on the street outside the house when I arrived. I drove around the block to the back alley and parked next to a garage, a few houses down. A bum stopped rifling through a garbage can long enough to eye me suspiciously. I reached in my pocket and took out a couple bucks. Waving them in my hand, I walked over to him and asked, "You see anybody around that gray house lately?"

"The houth where the guy got bumped off?" he asked with a lisp, most of his teeth missing.

"Yeah," I said and handed him one of the bills.

"Naw, ain't nobody been around thince the copth."

"You around here before the murder?"

He eyed the other bill I held with a lean, hungry look and furtively glanced from side to side. "Maybe."

"Did you see anybody around the house in the last week or so?"

He stared at the bill some more, licked his lips, and replied, "Only me an' Charlie."

"Did you see or talk to the guy who got killed?" I asked as I handed him the other dollar. I reached in my pocket and brought out two more bills.

"Dunno if it wath the thame guy got killed, but one night, 'bout a week ago, thith here guy comth in a cab. Cabbie dropped him off in the alley. Feller had thome bagth of food and liquor. Me and Charlie wath rootin' around back here. Thith fella called uth over and gave uth a bottle to help him carry hith bagth. Real nith guy," he said with a smile revealing his few brown-stained teeth.

"Is that the only time you saw him or talked to him?"

"Wath for me. Dunno 'bout Charlie. Me an' 'im got a room and thplit the bottle. I ain't theen Charlie thinth that night."

"Where can I find Charlie?"

He thought for a minute before replying, "If he ain't 'round theeth here parth, he'th probably holed up at one of the flophoutheth on theventy-fourth."

"What's his last name?"

"Dunno, just athk for Thoeless Charlie. Everybody'll know who ya mean."

I handed him the other two bucks and walked the alleyway to the house. The backyard had a broken-down weathered fence that hadn't seen paint in a long time. The gate, off the hinges, was lying in the unkempt grass. A small porch led up to a screen door sans screens. The door was locked when I tried the knob. I stepped back and kicked the door a couple inches below the lock. The wood easily splintered around the frame and the door flew open.

Everything was the same except for the stuff the police left behind after their investigation—cigarette butts, chewing gum, more empty booze bottles, and a whole host of dirty coffee cups. Upstairs, the police had marked the spot where I had discovered Joe. As I looked around the room, I tried to remember exactly how things were when I had found him.

Something tugged at my subconscious again but I couldn't grasp it. I thought back to our meeting, what Joe had said, and what had happened when I went to look for him when he didn't return from the kitchen. Then it hit me. Joe had said he was going to get more cigarettes from the kitchen, but there were none on him when I found him upstairs—a small point, probably an insignificant clue. He might have been sapped before he had a chance to fetch his cigarettes. There was another possibility, though. The killer had stolen my money. He could also have taken the cigarettes if Joe had retrieved them. The odd thing was I hadn't found the empty pack on Joe when I had searched him.

Chapter Eighteen

I didn't expect to find anything, but I searched the entire house anyway. There weren't any cigarettes in the kitchen cupboards when I looked earlier or now, nor were there any empty packs in the garbage. There were a couple books of matches from Roscoe's in the living room, nothing else. Suddenly I heard voices outside the front door. They didn't sound like the neighborhood kids playing in the street. Pulling a ragged, torn curtain aside, I peeked out and spotted Boots' boys, Sam and Tom, lugging their tonnage up the front steps. They pushed their way inside.

I beat a hasty retreat to the back door and waited. I heard Sam say, "This is a waste of time if ya ask me."

Tom replied, "Yeah, but Boots insisted. He'll skin us alive if we don't look."

"Okay, you take the upstairs and I'll start down here. Yell if ya find anythin'," Sam told his partner.

Quietly closing the back door behind me, I jumped off the stoop and dashed to my buggy. I climbed in, fired up the motor and took off down the alley. Nobody, including the old derelict, was around when I hit the street.

I drove around the block to see what car Boots' boys peddled. It wasn't hard to spot their black Cadillac parked at the corner. Nor was it difficult to see the black Dodge parked at the opposite end of the street.

"Well, look who's here," I muttered to myself and pulled out my gun. I had a score to settle with the crud behind that wheel. One way or another, the son-of-a-bitch was going to pay.

The neighborhood kids stopped playing ball long enough for me to drive through their impoverished ballpark. The driver threw his chariot into reverse when he saw me approach. He hit the gas and drove backwards towards the corner, his tires squealing in protest. I smashed my foot on the accelerator in pursuit. He wheeled around the corner, his momentum spinning the front end around when he braked and goosed the octane. His rear tires broke free sending up a cloud of burnt rubber before they regained traction and the car shot off like a scared rabbit. I was a split second too late in heading him off, but I got a better look at him this time than I had in Wisconsin.

He looked to be in his thirties. He sported dark wavy hair with an ugly jagged white scar over his left eyebrow. He wore the same dark sunglasses he had worn when he tried running me off the road earlier. The glasses were a distinguishing feature as generally only movie stars wore them. Again, I was struck by something vaguely familiar about him I couldn't place.

I goosed my chariot for all it was worth, but the Dodge easily pulled away from me. He made a right on Marquette and ran a stop light before he raced three more blocks and cut over on Western. I pursued him another dozen blocks or so, but keeping up was hopeless so I eased off the throttle.

Boots may have been telling the truth when he denied having me followed. Perhaps Butters could identify the driver from my description. Ever so slowly, the puzzle pieces were taking shape.

Traffic was stop-and-go all the way back downtown. My watch said noon when I finally swung my heep into a parking spot in the next block over from Frankie's Bar. Frankie was tending bar, but uncharacteristically he didn't give me his usual greeting when I perched on a stool in front of him. "How's it goin', Frankie?"

"Usual?" he asked laconically.

"Yeah, Butters in the back?"

He swallowed hard. "Geez Nick, don't you know? He's at St. Anthony's."

"A wedding or funeral?"

He looked at me like I had grown a second nose. "Not the church, the hospital. He's in the hospital. Somebody beat the shit out of him," he exclaimed.

It was my turn to drop my jaw. "How long ago?"

"Sometime last night. Eddie from the *Times* was just in here talkin' 'bout it. I left a message at your office as soon as I heard," he said earnestly.

"Shit," I said and tossed a buck on the bar.

I took Roosevelt Road to Ogden Avenue until I reached California and turned left driving over to 19th Street. The hospital parking lot was full, but I squeezed my heap between two wagons and lit out.

Running across the street, I made for the entrance. A matronly woman at the front desk directed me to the patient center where another nurse redirected me to the fourth floor. When I disembarked from the elevator, I followed the signs to the nurses' station where three nurses sat talking in hushed tones. When I cleared my throat, the nearest nurse looked at me with indifference and said, "Yes?"

"What room is Charles Butterworth in?"

She removed a clipboard from the edge of the top desk panel, scanned down the list of patients, and announced, "Room 404. But no visitors are allowed—doctor's orders."

"I understand," I said unctuously, "but I'm his brother and I just discovered he was here. Is there a doctor I can talk to?"

Her expression softened a bit, and she replied, "The doctor finished his rounds an hour ago. He'll be back early this evening. You need to complete the admittance forms since your brother was unconscious when admitted," she added as she withdrew a paper from a file, attached the parchment to a clipboard with a pencil and handed it to me.

"How is he?" I asked holding my breath.

She picked up Butters's file, studied the scribbling for a few seconds, and answered, "Hmm, he has a severely bruised sternum, sixth and seventh vertebrosternal fractured, separated costal cartilage, concussion, numerous contusions, and a possible skull fracture. He's in serious condition."

"Let me get this straight, his nose is broken, he's got two cracked ribs, a concussion, and lots of cuts and scrapes, is that right?"

She surveyed me circumspectly over her reading glasses. "Are you a doctor?"

"No, but I've had a lot of experience," I said offhandedly. "I better call sis. Is there a phone I can use?"

"There's a payphone down the hall," she said pointing to her left.

I thanked her and conveniently left the admission papers on the counter. A doorway at the end of the hall led to a stairwell. Taking the stairs two at a time, I came out on the third floor, walked to the end of the wing, where another set of stairs returned me to the fourth floor. The coast was clear when I cracked the stairwell door and peeked out. Butters's room was the second from the end.

His eyes were swollen shut and his face was a mess of purple bruises. When I pulled the sheet down covering his upper body, I saw deep scarlet welts peeking from under his tightly taped rib cage. Somebody had kicked the shit out of him as an afterthought.

Butters isn't going to tell me what, if anything, he had discovered for quite a while. There's one consolation to the whole business, though. If Butters was beaten to find out whom he was working for and he told them about me, how much worse could it be? Someone had already tried twice to kill me.

Chapter Nineteen

The slow boil inside me began roiling furiously as I hauled bunions back to my car. Somebody was going to pay in spades for Butters' going-over. My gun was biting into my stomach, so I slid it to my right side and steered my buggy westward. I stopped at an eatery on California to give my stomach acid something to gnaw on besides my clockworks. By the time I finished eating, my anger had subsided to a smoldering fire. It was time to pay Boots another call.

Part of me wanted Boots to provide me with any reason to take my aggression out on him and his boys. Butters had been making inquiries into the old mobsters. Someone in Boots' organization had to be responsible for his condition, so instead of continuing on to Boots' club, I pointed my car east and headed over to Albert Hewitt's warehouse again.

The same two hoods were playing cards when I entered. They weren't so casual about my sudden appearance as the first time I came a-calling. They jumped to their feet, but I already had my heater drawn and leveled at them.

"Easy fellows, easy. It's a friendly call. Turn around nice and slow and back up over there," I ordered with a wave of my roscoe.

After they were six feet from me, I ordered, "Take off your belts and drop them."

The shorter, stockier guy hesitated and reached to his side. At his first pause, I quickly closed the distance between us, grabbed a handful of his hair and smashed my gun into his temple as his arm whipped around, a .38 clutched in his mitt. He let out a sharp cry and dropped the piece before crumpling to the floor.

My gat was pointing at his partner before Shorty curled up asleep. "Your turn pally. The belt. Now!" I snarled.

He unloosened and pulled his belt from around his waist, letting it drop to the scarred wood floor. Facing him, I ordered, "Now remove your other gun by the barrel. Careful now!" He reached behind his waist and slowly extracted a long barreled Colt. He began to hand it to me.

"Uh-uh, on the floor."

When he bent over to place his gun on the floor, I stepped over and tapped him with the butt of my gun near the base of his skull. He kept going down until his body thudded into a heap, his face kissing the floor with a dull splat.

Shoving the goons' guns into my pants' pockets, I walked to Hewitt's office and threw open the door, gun braced in both hands. Hewitt looked up and dropped his jaw, making his long-horse face a caricature. He gurgled, "Wha-wha-what do you want?"

"Some straight answers or else you're going to get what your boys got."

"My boys? Are you nuts coming in here like this? Boots'll kill you when he finds out," he shrilled.

I stepped up to him and raked my gun sight across his skull, opening a red gash on his left temple. "Damn you," he screamed as he lifted his hand to his head, moaning when he touched his tender scalp. He withdrew his hand and stared at the blood in horror. Any second, I expected him to start crying.

"So you do report to Boots, eh? How did he take over your territory?"

He started to say something, but thought better of it as he stared at my .45 pointed at his right eyeball. "His boys come 'round, see, and ask if I heard about McClanahan. I tell 'em sure, I read the papers. Then they say the same thing's goin' to happen to me unless I sign on with Boots. I tell 'em to go to hell. Honest I did," he said and held up his palm.

"Yeah, I'm sure you're a real Boy Scout, Al. So then what?"

He scowled at my rejoinder and continued, "The guys tell me if I cooperate, I get to run da numbers as usual, and Boots will give me protection. I tell 'em to go to hell again, I got all the protection I need. I swear I did."

"Uh-huh, keep going," I urged.

He wiped the blood away from his brow again and stared at my rodney as I inched the cold steel closer to his face. "Well . . . then they tell me if I cooperate, Boots will pay me an extra hunert a month. All I gotta do is keep a couple of his boys handy and give him an accountin' of da month's biz. Honest."

"You get to keep all the numbers money and Boots pays you extra. Is that it?"

As he began to raise his hand, I cut him off, "Yeah, I know, that's the honest truth."

"Honest it is," he replied defensively.

"What kind of cars do your boys drive?"

"Cars? What's that gotta do with anything?"

I moved my gun until the barrel touched his nose, and he hurriedly answered, "Cars, yeah, uh, one's a Dodge and the other's a Ford, I think."

"Describe the Dodge?" I ordered.

"It's a brown job. I dunno the model."

While he was freewheeling with information, I continued, "You know any other guys in the numbers?"

"Know 'em by name, but only one I ever talk to is Pete."

"Pete who?"

"Pete Hamm, like da beer."

"Where's his operation?"

"It ain't his no more. He cashed out to Boots, too."

"That's all of it? Why is Boots paying you to stay and run your old numbers business?"

"I dunno, honest. I been thinkin' the same thing. It don't make no sense. It's got me plenty worried, too. Like maybe he's havin' his boys learn da biz and then he's plannin' to plant me anyhows."

"Makes sense," I agreed to make him squirm, even though I considered his conjecture unlikely given the simplicity of the numbers racket.

My affirmation made him wipe his brow again, and his already pallid complexion turned a pasty grey.

"I'd watch my back, if I were you," I advised, and hastily backed out of his office. The two lads were where I left them, unconscious. I unloaded their guns and laid them on the floor before I hustled through the front room and out the door.

I discovered Hamm lived on Hubbard in the near west side when I stopped and looked him up in Ma Bell's telephone directory. It was a little blue bungalow with white trim. A tiny neat strip of grass adorned the front, and flowers were set in large pots on the small porch. A white five-foot high wood fence encircled the cozy little abode. I walked around the block to the alley and checked out Hamm's garage. Peering through the window, I saw a black Packard parked inside.

I walked back to the entrance to his bungalow. The gate wasn't locked when I tried the latch. A small man in his sixties wearing a blue dress shirt and grey slacks answered when I yanked the doorbell.

"Mr. Hamm, I presume?"

"Yes?"

"I'd like a minute of your time," I said and flashed him my license.

He opened the door and waved me into a small, comfortable living room. He turned off a Philco radio sitting on a table in the corner before inviting me to sit down on a new sofa. "Now what do you want to know?" he asked and sat down in an artsy chair of mahogany and woven cane.

"I'll cut to the chase, Mr. Hamm. I know you ran numbers on the West Side until recently when Boots Handel took over your operation. Would you tell me about the transaction, sir?"

He got a kick out of my formality judging from his grin. He looked like such a nice old man—his small feet encased in a pair of leather slippers, and his small frame engulfed in the big chair. I couldn't help but return his grin. "I'm afraid there's not much to tell young man. Mr. Handel purchased my business, now I'm retired."

"Did he threaten you? Is that why you sold out?"

"Heavens no, he was more than generous in his offer."

"Why do you think he paid you so much?"

"None of my business. The man wants to pay, who am I to ask why? Besides I'm not getting any younger."

"None of us are," I agreed. "Was the transaction straightforward?"

"Yes," he answered laconically.

"Anything peculiar or out of the ordinary about the transaction or how Mr. Handel handled matters?"

"As I said, nothing," he answered.

I wasn't going to get anything more out of this old bird, so I said, "Thanks for your time, Mr. Hamm," and made for the door.

"You're welcome," he returned without making an effort to see me out.

An idea began to take shape as I weaved through traffic toward my office. The time was between the afternoon shoppers and supper crowd, making for plenty of parking spots in my block. I didn't see any cops as I walked into the building, but I decided to play it safe and take the stairs. When I reached my office, a couple of messages were stuck under the door.

The first message was from Frankie saying Butters was at St. Anthony's. The second message was from Bobby asking if I would play with the band again. *He must be a glutton for punishment.* Foot leather slapped on the marble outside my office and the door opened. I made a grab for my gun, but stopped when I saw the blue uniform.

"You might try knocking," I snarled.

"Lieutenant Powers told me to bring you in," my captor said in a stern voice. "Make with the gun," he ordered.

I placed my .45 in his hand, and cordially said, "Lead the way."

"You first," he retorted with an unnecessary prod.

He was quiet and careful, keeping a wary eye on me. He stood a safe distance away to eliminate any hijinks I might consider. Only after he slammed shut the rear door of the squad car did he speak again, "Lieutenant told me to tell you your time was up."

"Tell Powers he can . . . ah, forget it. I'll tell Junior myself," I said irritably.

When we arrived at the State Street precinct headquarters, the cop ushered me upstairs to the second floor. The marble lined hallway echoed every step as we walked to Powers' office. Junior sat behind an old oak desk piled high with files. A metal wastebasket sat in the corner filled with crumpled papers. File cabinets lined one wall and the place reeked of cigarette smoke.

Without looking up, Powers said, "Sit down and shut up Verriet. Bring us some java and a coupla of sinkers, Harry," he said to my attendant.

Harry returned in a few moments, set the coffee and donuts on the desk and departed. Powers took a sip and quickly removed the cup from his lip. "Dammit, must be a new pot, burnt my tongue."

I let his hospitality and remark go unheeded. This was Powers' show; I sat quietly, dunked my donut and ate in silence. Minutes ticked by without a word, only the sound of Powers' scribbling broke the silence.

He vanquished all thoughts of my taking a siesta saying, "All right, Verriet, I want it all and I want it fast. If I think for one minute you're holding out on me, you're going downstairs," meaning he'd have me booked and jugged.

I laid everything out for him, including pulling my shirt up and showing him my bandaged wound. When I finished, he grunted and said, "It stinks. You get a license number on the Dodge?"

"No, the guy didn't have plates."

"Well, at least that's something," he said, and picked up the phone on his desk. "Marsha, see if either Ray Stepson or Bob Wilks is in and have them come to my office pronto." He turned back to me and said, "All right, where were we? Oh yeah," he paused before continuing, "Why in hell would Boots hire you and then try to kill you? It doesn't make sense. And I refuse to believe one of the guys whose territory he took over would bother with you, no matter how big a pain in the ass you are."

"Unless he's using me like you are," I growled.

"I'm supposed to feel sorry for you?" he asked sardonically.

"Yeah, everybody uses everybody don't they? I finally figured that out after I got my ass shot up in France."

Powers' eyes opened wider, and he said, "Didn't know you were in the war. My son died over there."

"A big part of me did, too," I said bitterly. "You want to know what really stinks, Lieutenant?"

"You don't have to tell me, I read the paper, too."

Our conversation was interrupted when a tall, lanky, red-haired guy walked in and plopped down in the chair next to me. "Wilks is working a prostitution ring, so I'm elected. What's up?"

"Thanks for coming," Powers said. "Ray, this is Nick Verriet. He's a private dick. I'd like you to hear what he has to say and give me your two-cents worth. The case he's working ties in with two homicides we're investigating and at least one other attempted murder." He shifted his attention to me and ordered, "Give him the goods, same as you did me."

"Everything?" I asked.

"Yeah, from the beginning," Powers replied.

I laid it all out again. Ray interrupted me a few times with questions and when I finished he eased back in the chair.

"Everything fits from our side. You peg Boots for McClanahan's shooting?" he asked Powers.

"Yeah, but we can't prove it."

"Sure as shit Boots has got something in the works. He's sewn up the numbers from the near North Side to Dies' in the south. My guess is he's waiting until he's got a lock on all the clients, then he's gonna lower the boom. He's on the trolley—smart. That's why he's keepin' the old brass in place."

"And you figure his records were stolen? That's what he's looking for?" Powers asked Ray.

"Sure. It's the only thing that can nail him. Otherwise, all we can do is go after the bosses he's kept on. Maybe that's his plan," Ray said with sudden inspiration. "He's keeping the former guys in place as insulation. Either that or he's got something planned for a big switchover. He's going after economies of scale—bringing all of Chi's numbers under one house."

From the look on Powers' face, he was skeptical of Ray's theory, but didn't say so. "Maybe," said Powers, "let's keep close on this one, Ray. If Boots is going to clean house, we'll need to work together."

Powers dismissed Ray after Ray assured him he'd keep him informed of any developments. Powers gave me a hard stare and said, "I'll probably regret this, but you can go, Verriet. Before you do, remember I've got the D.A. breathing hard down my neck and time is running out. He's coming up for re-election this fall. You know what that means?"

"Yeah, I'm an expendable, just like your son," I said pointedly.

My remark hit a sore spot. His face took on the countenance of a very tired old man. I was sorry I had lashed out at him as I hit the street. At least I had him off my back for a while. I suspected the only reason he gave me a break was due to my military kinship with his son.

Chapter Twenty

The late afternoon shadows lulled the city's denizens to a dulled anticipation of better things to come in the evening when I returned to my office. I called the hospital and waited on the line five minutes before being connected to the nurses' station. It took some persuading to loosen up the nurse's tongue when I asked how Butters was doing. She didn't want to give out any information to a stranger. Lucky for me, she was a different nurse than the one I had talked to earlier so I reiterated my spiel about being his brother from out of town—how I'd just found out he was in the hospital from his co-worker.

She informed me Butters was recovering satisfactorily from an operation to fix his nose and his x-rays had come back negative—he didn't have a fractured skull, only a concussion. I thanked the nurse and hung up when she asked me for family information. They'd be on alert the next time someone made any inquiries, but I'd worry about that when the time came. It would be a couple days before Butters would be in any kind of shape to talk and by then I'd have figured out another way to circumvent the hospital's bureaucracy.

I picked up Frankie's and Bobby's messages lying on the floor where I had dropped them after Powers' man had grabbed me earlier. The day was wearing on, and since I had no immediate plans, I decided to see Bobby and decompress a little by playing with the band again. First, I needed some nourishment. I'd been running on high for too long and already had to tighten my belt a notch since beginning this case.

I settled for Schaller's Pump eatery on South Halstead. The Ambrosia Brewery was next door and they ran a not-so-secret hose from the brewery to the bar. Nobody made pot roast like Schaller's cook, you could cut the meat with a fork. After a couple of cold beers and two helpings of meat with boiled onions, potatoes, and carrots, I paid, and headed over to Roscoe's.

As soon as I walked through the door, Sam braced me and told me Boots wanted to see me. He grabbed my arm above the elbow in an iron grip and marched me to the office. Nudging me inside, he shut the door behind us, leaned back against the wall by the door and began to play a tune with his razor.

Boots looked up from his books. "Whaddya got?"

"Nothin' but a sore ribcage, my best friend's in the hospital, and the bulls are breathing down my neck like a pack of hungry jackals."

"That's all?"

"Yeah, if you call getting shot 'all.' Me, I call it enough," I snapped.

Boots frowned and gave Sam a look. Sam shrugged his shoulders and Boots refocused his attention to me. "You got drilled, huh?"

"Yeah, if you don't believe me take a gander," I replied, and pulled my shirt out of my pants and let him lamp my bandages. "Satisfied?" I asked peevishly.

Nonplused, he asked, "Get a look at the guy?"

"Naw," I feigned, "it was too dark."

With each passing second, Boots became more agitated. I sat and stared at him in silence. He shook his head from side to side like an angry bull. "You must be gettin' close for somebody to plug you."

"Uts-nay," I replied.

"Whaddya mean?"

"I mean, I quit. Hell, what you paid me will barely cover my doctor bills. I'm in business to make money, not to go around being a target for every loose cannon with a grudge against you. Your geetus isn't going to do me a helluva a lot of good when I'm six feet under, or if my carcass lands in the hoosegow."

"I thought Joe was your friend and you wanted to find his killer," he challenged.

"Yeah, well I've had a change of heart. Let the cops put some of my tax money to work and find him. I've had enough."

My act gave Boots pause to think. After a few seconds reflection, he said, "Wait out in the bar for a bit. Tell Vinny the drinks are on me."

After I closed the office door, I put my ear to the door and listened. Boots and Sam were carrying on a heated discussion, but the door was made of solid wood and I only caught an occasional word. One thing was clear, Boots was not happy somebody had tried to kill me. That made two of us.

Chapter Twenty-one

Bobby was nursing a drink at the bar with a forlorn look. He waved me over.

"Man, can we use you tonight, Nick. Practice was lemons today. The beat was way off, and Chuck didn't show."

"Probably scored, that's the way with users," I said as I caught the bartender's attention and waved my index finger around in a circle.

"Yeah, kid's a damn good player, if only he'd clean up."

"Is he hooked up with Gale? I heard they were a couple somewhere down the line."

The bartender brought our drinks. When he returned to reading his paper at the other end of the bar, Bobby replied, "I don't think so, but it's hard to tell, Nick. She mothers him and he gets jealous when any guy pays her attention, but you know how riding the horse is. He's all over the map when he's hurtin'. All he really cares about is where his next junk is coming from."

"Yeah, I know how it is," I said reflexively shaking off the all too familiar queasy feeling. "Did Chuck come over with Gale from Detroit or did Boots bring him over?"

"Got me. All I know is Chuck signed on with Joe and then Gale showed up a few days later. Why don't you ask Boots?"

"I'd hate to get anybody in hot water. If they've got something going it's probably not important anyway. So what's on for tonight?"

Before he could answer, we were interrupted by Sam, "Boots says he's finished with you for now shamus, but don't plan on going too far if you know what's good for you." With that exclamation, he heeled it back to Boots' office.

With a nervous look, Bobby ushered me over to the bandstand and ran down the song list.

"Let's switch *Am I Blue* and *My Man* around to vary the keys better," I suggested.

"Yeah, that is better," he said with a head nod.

We made a few more tweaks to liven things up and then it was time for me to warm up. This time, I had brought my own trusty guitar and everything went snazzy. We played a few numbers to the gathering crowd, warming things up a bit. Then it was time for the first set. The band picked up on my enthusiasm and we began hitting on all cylinders. By the time we finished, everyone was loose and the improvisations began to jive amongst the players. Bobby and I really cooked during *I've Found a New Baby.*

The second session was the cat's meow as well. Bobby introduced Gale after the lead-in numbers. She appeared on stage wearing a shimmering midnight blue, body-hugging dress that looked like someone had dipped her into a barrel of oil. Low cut in the front and back, she was a stunner. She had her black hair styled differently, longer than a pageboy on the sides, but retaining the neat straight bangs of the previous evening. Her hair reflected the blue from her dress under the soft spot-lights. Bright red lipstick added the perfect touch.

She sashayed over to my station, gave me a come-on look and leaned toward me as she sang. The position gave me a front row seat to a dazzling display of her heaving chest as she belted out the next couple of tunes. I found it nearly impossible to concentrate on the music and watch her at the same time, so I stared at the fretboard until we finished playing.

Gale was *on* tonight and she knew it. She was a fast learner. She anticipated the changes better, and had a little fun with the boys throwing in a bit of skat here and there. After the set, she waited at the bar, a drink ready for me when I squeezed my chassis in next to hers.

"You're quick on the uptake. I'm impressed."

"Thanks, Nick. You're fitting in like an old glove, why don't you play all the time?"

"Maybe I will. It feels great to whoop it up with the boys, again." I replied with a smile.

"I have the suspicion you'd do all right on your own," she retorted.

"Not like you, doll. Hell, if you had the right connections in the movie business, you'd have them eating out of your hand."

"You really think so, Nick?" she asked earnestly with eyes ablaze.

"Know so. All we can hope for is jazz to keep going. Who knows what tomorrow's music will be. I can't imagine anything that'll swing more than hot jazz, though."

"I'm like you. Hot jazz is the cat's pajamas. I grew up listening to polkas and fox trots. My old man used to take my mother dancing to the local German restaurant when I was a kid. I remember the first time I heard jazz—a neighbor was playing records next door. It was summer and they had their windows open. I went over and sat under their window, listening to the music all afternoon. It's been in my blood ever since.

"I made my ex pay for singing lessons. I told him either he coughed up the dough or I'd go to the newspapers and tell them all his dirty little secrets I learned about him and his holier-than-thou family from top to bottom. I knew I would need something to depend on besides my looks once I left him. Little did I know then how right I was, and little did I know what a kick it was to sing on stage.

"Nothing beats performing at an upscale club—like here— especially with the lights turned down low and I sing an intimate number to offset the energy of the hot stuff. Boots might be a gangster, but he sure knows the entertainment biz."

"Yeah, I know what you mean. There's something special about playing off each other. The mood is special in this kind of joint."

"Ooo, Nick, when we're clicking I feel chills up my spine." She said with a slight shiver and studied me for a moment with her gorgeous hazel eyes gleaming brightly. "Are we going to hook up after the show?"

Just like that, she laid it out. "Sounds good to me," I said with a dry rasp and gulped the last of my drink. "Except my place is a wreck, how about yours tonight?"

107

She laughed lightly. "Silly, I don't mind, but my place is berries."

Bobby blew a note to cue us for the next set and I rejoined the band as Gale went to her dressing room to wait for us to play the usual warm-up numbers. The last two sets went by quickly—the week-end crowd was most appreciative. The atmosphere became heavy with cigarette smoke and I had to sip my drink between numbers to avoid choking. By the time we finished, everybody in the band was satisfied with the night's performance. Bobby was especially complimentary to me. He seconded Gale's opinion that I should become a permanent fixture in the group.

April, the coat-check gal came around the corner and gave me a big smile that quickly vanished when Gale grabbed me by the arm and gave me a kiss. With Gale's kiss, April gave me the kiss-off, did an about face, and marched away without a word.

Gale left to change and returned in a few moments wearing a pair of silk slacks right out of the Arabian Nights and a loose red blouse. We were both too pumped-up with adrenaline to call the evening quits when we climbed into my jalopy. I drove to the South Side and squeezed my flivver between two other cars in an alleyway lined by old brick buildings.

"I've got a surprise for you. See that joint over there?" I asked and pointed to the back of a two-story brick building.

"Yeah, what about it?" she replied.

"It's the Dreamland Café where the real jazz guys come to jam all night. Let's go and unwind," I suggested.

"I'm wound up, too, Nick, but I was thinking of another way to unwind," she said with a salacious look.

I took her arm in mine, pressed her curvaceous framework against me. "There's plenty of time for that later. Let's see how the old pros do it, huh?"

"You mean there's another way?" she joked.

We went through a back door painted a dull black. Inside, a small flight of steps at the end of a dimly lit hall led to another door. The door was locked, so I bruised my knuckles on it and a big, heavyset colored gonzo cracked open a peek-a-boo door slot.

He surveyed me briefly before his attention focused on Gale. With a nod of his head, he opened the door for us to enter. The place was crowded elbow to elbow. The air was dense with smoke, not all of it from cigarettes. We weaved our way through the packed house to the small bar at the back of the room.

We wedged ourselves into a standing room only spot at the end of the bar and I ordered us drinks. The bartender gave me a grin, nodded at Gale, and rolled his eyes skyward when he set down our drinks. I knew him and returned his leer with a wink as I flipped him one of the large deuce notes.

Gale intently studied the female singer. I recognized a couple of guys playing on the tiny stage. I looked around and spotted a few other familiar faces. We had another drink and I held Gale in my arms in front of me as we listened to the band. She rapturously swayed to the beat when the band swung slowly. At half past three, I was tired of standing and suggested we leave. Gale nodded in ready agreement.

She lived in an old brownstone house divided into four apartments. She had the place upstairs on the left. The small living room was sparsely furnished, but the few furniture pieces she did have were tasteful and the golden sand colored walls warmed up the place. She kicked off her heels after locking the door behind us, exclaiming, "My pups are killing me."

"Lie down and I'll give them a massage," I offered.

She grabbed my hand and led me to her bedroom. "You always know just the right thing to say," she said as she unclasped her pantoons, slid them down and kicked them off. She removed her blouse, and stretched her hull down on the bed in her clinging silk underalls. Her alluring epidermis made my short hairs stand at attention.

I followed suit and removed my clothes down to my underwear. She gasped and sat up when she glimmed my bandages.

Wide-eyed, she asked, "What happened to you?"

"Somebody shot me this morning."

"Wha-what?"

"Uh-huh, somebody shot me in my apartment's garage."

"Is that why you didn't want to go to your place tonight?"

"You've got me," I agreed abashedly.

"Nick, you should have told me. I wouldn't have kept you out. Are you okay?" she asked with a concerned look.

"I'm fine. The doc gave me some pills, and with the alcohol I drank, I'm feeling no pain," I said with a smile.

"Are you sure we should be doing this?"

"Would you stop acting like my mother and lay down," I ordered and gave her a gentle push back into her pillows.

I grabbed one of her feet and kneaded it between my hands. She "oohed" and "aahed" under my ministrations. Slowly, I worked my way up, rubbing her calf muscles and then her thighs, one at a time, between my hands, running them up and down while kneading the muscles.

When I finished, she grabbed my shoulders and pulled me down on top of her. We knew what to expect of each other and the anticipation made our lovemaking better than before, more mutually satisfying. She curled up into my right arm afterward, and I thought she had fallen asleep until she interrupted my thoughts. "Nick, I've been thinking about what you said tonight—you know, about jazz and all?"

"Uh-huh," I acknowledged.

"If you find Boots' dough, let's go to Europe. There's bound to be some great opportunities there."

"It's a thought," I replied as she snuggled closer and began rubbing her leg up and down mine, challenging me to a rematch.

Chapter Twenty-two

Sunday

Gale and I enjoyed a late breakfast at a neighborhood eatery. She wore no makeup, and had slipped on a simple black and white dress that would have looked plain on most women, but her curves made the dress come alive. Something about her freshly scrubbed face turned her into a picture of innocence.

After we finished our pancakes, I eased back in my chair.

She lit a cigarette, studied my face, and said, "Penny for your thoughts."

"I'm thinking about what you said last night."

"You mean Europe?"

"Uh-huh. Did you mean it?"

"Of course I meant it. Why else would I have said it?"

"Would you still go with me if I didn't find Boots' money?" I asked skeptically.

"I don't know, Nick," she answered, surprising me by her candor. "I'm not very good at saving money. What would we live on?"

"What I've got wouldn't last us through the summer," I admitted. "We'd have to find work. I know some jazz guys over there, though. I think we'd be able to make out okay, but it might take a while to get jake."

She considered what I'd said. "At least it would be a change of scenery. I've never been out of the Midwest, have you?"

"Yeah, I was stationed in England for a spell and then fought over in France and Belgium."

"Is that how you got all those scars?"

"Some of them," I replied and switched the subject. "Gale, how did you happen to hook up with Boots?"

"I was working at a dive in Detroit, a real hole-in-the-wall. One night he sent me a note asking me to join him after the last set. He introduced himself as the owner of a big club uptown called The Rocket. Bands performed on the weekends, and small jazz groups were featured during the week. He offered me three times my salary. About a year later, Boots sold out to a big promoter who strictly wanted a restaurant, so I went back to a small juice joint again. I jumped at the chance to leave Detroit when he called and offered me my old job and pay here in Chicago."

"On the level, did Boots ever try to saddle up next to you?"

"Nope. I made things clear to him up front that I didn't mix business and pleasure," she said assuredly.

"Smart," I said, "but something bothers me, Gale. If Boots is your meal ticket, why do you want to screw him and take his money?"

"Look, for one thing, Boots is a crook," she replied tartly. "He's running numbers here. In Detroit it was numbers and women. I don't owe him a thing and I'm sick and tired of living hand to mouth. I'm willing to take the risk to get out from under once and for all. I thought you were in the same boat," she said pugnaciously.

I dismissed her challenge. "Why not marry some rich guy? With your looks you can snag somebody easily."

She shrugged her shoulders, and looked at me intently. Then she let down her defenses. "I'll let you in on a little secret, Nick. I already told you I was married before, but what I didn't tell you was I was only seventeen at the time and my husband was from one of the wealthiest families in Detroit. The whole time I was his little obedient wife I felt like I was on display. I had to act a certain way in front of his friends and family. He treated me like an object, one of his prize possessions. I'm surprised he didn't mount my head up on the wall of his study with the rest of his trophies. It was a nightmare; his family despised me for marrying their pride and joy. When he grew tired of me, the heel rigged the divorce. His family had all the lawyers and judges in their pocket. Except for those voice lessons, I ended up with nothing but a big, fat attorney's fee. I learned the hard way."

"So how do I fit in?"

She gave me a quizzical look. "Tell you the truth, Nick, I'm not sure. I mean you don't fit in. Uh, no—that's not what I mean. I'm all confused," she said and blushed. "You see, I was keeping my distance, waiting for the right guy. I didn't think anything about you in that way until you played with the band. Then, well, everything changed. You bowled me over with your playing, and when we did those solo numbers together, something happened to me I never experienced before. It's hard for me to put into words, but I guess I fell for you that night."

"And now?" I implored.

"Now, everything's up in the air," she replied laughing lightly. "Nothing is working out how I planned it."

"Yeah, I know what you mean."

"I need to do some grocery shopping this afternoon. How about coming by later and I'll fix us dinner?"

"Now you're on the trolley, dolly. I'll come around six, how's that?"

"Better make it seven. I'm going to throw a roast in the oven."

I paid our bill and we strolled to her home. I felt strange walking with her. Here I was falling in love all over again with Teri, and now I was hedging my bets—talking about leaving for Europe with Gale.

I pushed everything out of my mind as I drove home amidst a bright sunny day with a light cool breeze blowing off the lake. *Maybe I'll take a drive up Lake Shore Drive*, I thought as I pulled into my garage space. Then I remembered what happened the last time I entered the garage, and kept low as I climbed out of my car. Nobody tried to kill me as I made my way to the elevator. Nevertheless, I carefully inserted my key into my apartment door lock, pushed the door open, and took a quick peek inside before I entered.

After a long hot shower, I felt like a new man. My wound bled a little from the shower, and last night's workout with Gale didn't help any. My skin was extremely tender as I patted the area dry. I slowly changed the dressing and taped new bandages in place. Finished with my side, I decided to take out my stitches. They itched like hell. I had to dig into my scalp with a pair of scissors to snip and yank them out. Afterward, I took an aspirin powder and slipped on a pair of slacks.

The telephone rang and when I answered it, Teri said, "Nick, where have you been? I've been trying to reach you since four this morning. Somebody tried to break in."

"Are you okay?"

"Yeah, just scared. I heard somebody try to force the backdoor open. It woke me up. I made a lot of noise, and guess I frightened them away. That's when I first tried calling you."

"I've been working on finding Joe's killer," I said weakly.

"All night?"

"Yeah, I was shot yesterday."

"Oh my gosh. Are you alright, Nick?"

"Yeah, just another scar. Nothing to worry about. Teri, do you have a gun?"

"Joe kept one somewhere, a little .22, I think."

"See if you can find it. I'll be there in two shakes."

"Hurry, will you, Nick? I'm so scared I'm shivering."

"Have a drink. I'm on my way, honey," I said and hung up.

Luckily, I didn't encounter any cops en route as I recklessly sped to Teri's. My flivver's brakes squealed in protest as I pulled up to the curb in front of her bungalow. Dashing up the stairs, I yanked the door ringer, but nobody answered. I pulled the bell again and when no one answered, I tried the knob and began pounding on the door. A faint sound came from the rear of the house and I heard a car start up. A sick feeling crept up my spine as I ran around the corner toward the back.

The screen door hung open, the rear door wasn't closed either. I whipped out my gun and held it in front of me. Slowly, I shuffled noiselessly through the door into the kitchen and paused. Listening, I didn't hear a thing but muffled traffic sounds. Pots and pans lay strewn about and cupboard doors and drawers were open. I waited and listened a moment before I continued into the living room, looking for Teri and expecting the worst.

The place looked just like the last time somebody had searched it. Teri was always neat; she wouldn't have left a mess like this.

114

Somebody had broken in and ransacked her place again. All I could think about was Teri's safety. I'd never forgive myself if she got hurt while I had been playing house with Gale. I continued my slow, methodical search, going from room to room.

The living room was clear. I sucked in air as I walked expectantly toward Joe and Teri's bedroom. A glance around the door revealed nothing and I breathed a sigh of relief. I called out her name again, but there was no answer. I walked all the way into the bedroom and that's when I saw the leg sticking out from the other side of the bed.

Chapter Twenty-three

A moment of panic hit me until I lamped pants and a man's brogan. I walked around the bed and spotted Chuck. He was deader than a canned sardine. Swearing under my breath, I bent over and examined him, his head lying in a pool of blood. Shot in the back of the head, the entry hole was small, the kind made by a .22. The bullet had exited through his right eye socket. I'd seen a lot worse during the war, but he made for a grim sight lying there staring through one eye into the great beyond.

Chuck wasn't going anywhere, so I continued my search. After I checked the other bedroom, I proceeded to the basement. There was no sign of Teri. The purse she always carried was missing, and when I checked the garage, her car was gone. *Was that Teri I heard driving off when I was at the front door?*

Only the main floor was in disorder. *Did Teri catch Chuck in the act and shoot him with Joe's gun? It sure looks that way.* I returned to Chuck's body and went through his pockets, but didn't find anything of interest except a piece of paper with Teri's address on it. His body held a last bit of warmth. He had to have been killed almost at the time of my arrival.

Sitting on a corner of the bed, I thought about what to do. If I called the cops, Powers was sure to suspect Teri, if he didn't pin the murder on me. If I didn't call the cops, I was running the risk of somebody in the neighborhood spotting my heap. In that case, I'd be in a worse jam than if I had called the cops. No matter how I turned it over in my mind, I was in a fix. The noose was drawing tighter and if I didn't find Joe's killer soon, it would be my neck stretched.

The telephone receiver was off the cradle in the living room. I pressed the cradle a couple times until I heard the operator. Powers wasn't in when I asked for him and neither was Ray. I had to settle for a Sergeant named Ferguson. I gave him a quick run-down on the murder and told him Powers would want to know about it as it pertained to a case he was working. He insulted my intelligence by telling me not to leave. By the time

Ferguson arrived, I was seriously doubting the wisdom of reporting the murder.

Ferguson was a big bruiser, a tough Irishman, about six-two; he must have weighed two-twenty if he weighed an ounce. He looked over the body for a few seconds before he called for assistance. In another hour, the place was a zoo between the photographers, news reporters, and neighbors.

About the time the newsboys dashed off to write their stories, Powers marched in the front door. He took one look at me and shook his head sadly from side to side as if he was sorry for me. I accompanied him into the bedroom.

"Do you know him?"

"Yes and no. He's, I mean, he *was* one of the band members at Boots' place. His name is Chuck. I don't know his last name. One of the band members introduced him to me a few days ago. That's all I know about him, except the fact he's a user like Honey."

Powers harrumphed at my statement and kneeled down. He unbuttoned one of Chuck's shirtsleeves. "A drug user all right." He held up the arm so I could see the rows of needle marks. Then he tilted Chuck's head and examined the wound. "Looks like a .22."

"Yeah," I agreed and held up my gun. "As you can see, it wasn't mine."

He ignored me and continued to examine the body. "You find anything on him?"

"Didn't look."

"And how did you happen to be here?" Before I answered, an errant newsman waltzed into the room, and Powers said to me, "It's a bit crowded in here. Why don't we go someplace else and talk?"

We made our way, weaving to the kitchen through the growing number of curious neighbors gathered in the living room where Ferguson was taking their statements. We settled into a couple of chairs and I related the events beginning with Teri's phone call. I failed to mention Teri telling me about Joe's gun.

117

"Was Mrs. Marcus here when you arrived?" he asked while studiously studying my face.

"No, nobody was here, but as I've said, I heard what sounded like a car starting up from out back."

"How long did it take you from the time of the call to get here?"

"About thirty minutes," I answered.

"Did the Marcus's have a gun?"

"I don't know for sure."

"What do you mean, 'for sure'," he snapped.

"I don't know for sure if the Marcus' owned a gun. Joe never mentioned one to me, but that doesn't mean he didn't have one," I retorted.

"What time did she call you?"

I glanced at my watch. "About half past ten, I guess. I didn't really check. I just beat it the hell over here."

"You and the missus got something going?" Powers spat accusingly.

My ears turned hot and my blood pressure shot up like a skyrocket. "Why you miserable bastard," I replied in outrage. "I've told you how close Joe, Teri, and I were before I went overseas. We were best friends."

Powers squinted at me, and said, "Me thinks thou dost protest too much."

Great, now I've got a cop quoting me Shakespeare. But I had to admit Powers' years of dealing with people had honed his detection skills into a fine art. Warning myself to watch my step, I forced myself to calm down. "Teri was like a sister to me, Lieutenant. I feel very protective of her."

"What do you mean 'was,'" he asked watching my facial expression carefully.

"Just what I said," I replied defensively, "after the war, I hardly saw her or Joe."

We went back and forth for another twenty minutes until Ferguson popped his head in and announced, "All through, Lieutenant. We found the slug, a .22." He glanced at his notes and continued, "He was shot from close range, only a couple inches away, judging from the powder burns. The bullet entered the lower right occipital and exited through his right superior orbital fissure."

Powers interrupted, "Whoever shot him was probably right-handed."

"Not necessarily," Ferguson rejoined, "I remember the Bakes' case where—"

"I know, I know, I'm working percentages," Powers countered testily.

The two men exchanged information while I remained dolefully quiet. It sure looked like Teri had caught Chuck flatfooted and shot him with Joe's gun. If so, I was partially to blame for asking her to find his gun. Like everything else in this case, nothing was working out. Somebody was pulling the strings, and I was tired of being a puppet.

After Ferguson ushered the last of the onlookers out, Powers returned his attention to me. "I think you're covering for the wife, Verriet."

"Think what you want, but I don't know where she is."

"It's not what I think, it's what the D.A. will think. Five will get you ten, he's gonna tell me to bring you in."

"Do what you have to do," I capitulated, "but I suspect the body count is going to keep climbing. You'd be doing me a favor at this point to lock me up so the D.A. can't blame the next murder on me."

"Dammit, man, what do you know you're not telling me?"

"I don't know from nothin'."

Powers swore some more. "What the hell makes you so certain there's going to be another murder?"

"It's obvious, isn't it? Chuck was looking for whatever Boots lost. And that means Joe didn't tell whoever killed him where it was. The word is out and every mother's son is probably trying to find whatever it is, because whatever *it* is will either make them wealthy and/or give them a strangle hold on Boots. It's turning into one hell of a balled up mess. First, it was Joe, and now it's

Chuck. Pretty soon the morgue is going to fill up with guys representing different mobs, all at odds to see who can claim the prize."

"Begads, Verriet, what did you and the Marcuses start?"

"Like I said, I don't know from nothing. I was only called to help an old friend find Joe. Now every cheap thug is taking pot shots at me, your threatening to lock me up, and the cherry on top of this shit sundae is I have a mob boss lamping my every move. Not to mention the fact that the D.A.'s up for election and I'm his poster boy to shoe him in for another term because the cops in this city can't solve a murder on their own. I've half a mind to leave town until the shooting's over. You and the D.A. can play janitor and clean up afterward."

"Watch your trap or you'll be riding in the meat wagon with your pal Chuck. You're not going anywhere, got that?" he snarled.

"All right, let's put our cards on the table and help each other. We're not getting anywhere exchanging threats. You've already used me as a decoy, and it's what I expected. Don't you think it's time you leveled with me?"

"That's a lark, me holding out on you. You're the one holding the cards," he retorted hotly.

"Every card I've been dealt so far has turned out to be a joker, and I'm sure as hell not the dealer."

"Bullshit, I've had enough of this. Come on, I'm hauling you in."

"Aren't you forgetting the most important point about Chuck?"

"You mean him being a drug user?"

"Bingo, give the man a cigar. Chuck was hooked and all somebody who's hooked cares about is his next high. That means Chuck was either looking for H, money to buy it, or something he could use to get it."

Powers settled back in his chair and thought aloud, saying, "I've thought this case was about dope from the beginning, Verriet, but Boots has never dealt in drugs so let's rule it out for the time being. That leaves money or Boots' books. Money is easy, but going after Boots' books is another story. I can't see the skinny bastard that's lying dead in the next room having the balls to extort from Boots if he had found his books."

"You're all wet! The last time I saw Chuck, he was hurting. He'd have sold his mother to make a score. And another thing, whoever shot Chuck knew him. These old wood floorboards creak worse than a rusted-out jalopy's springs. The hair around the hole in the back of his head is singed down to the follicles. Like Sergeant Ferguson indicated, a .22 would have to be held damn close to burn like that."

Powers sat silently and agitated his little grey cells until Ferguson marched into the kitchen. "The wagon's loaded and the newsboys have all vamoosed. Do you want me to stay?"

Powers looked at me, shook his head, and said, "You can leave, Sergeant. I'll have Smithy secure the joint."

"I'd like to make a quick phone call before you take me in, Junior. You can listen in if you want," I asserted.

"Go to hell. Scram before I change my mind. The D.A.'s gonna drill me a new one for this. But get this, and get it straight. You report to me morning, noon, and night, you hear?"

"Loud and clear," I affirmed.

"I don't hear from you and out goes the word, got it? And if you see Mrs. Marcus, you bring her in. If I find out you two have cooked something up, I'll personally pull the lever in Joliet."

He finished the hard guy routine and I got the hell out of there. There wasn't a doubt in my mind the D.A. was going to have Powers collar me once this murder reached his desk. As of that moment, I was living on borrowed time—barely enough to change my address to Stateville Prison in Joliet.

Chapter Twenty-four

I figured I'd stop off and give Boots the latest news about Chuck. As I crossed the river and followed Wacker Drive around to the west, I saw someone who looked like Teri walk out of Roscoe's. "It can't be," I said under my breath. She climbed into a white Dodge and I exclaimed, "Damn it to hell, it *is* Teri," in disbelief. *What is she doing at* Roscoe's*?*

She turned on Randolph, and I hightailed after her. Traffic was light, but the stoplights didn't cooperate with my agenda. I was trapped behind two cars at the next light and by the time I turned on Randolph her car was no longer in sight. *She must have turned, but which way?* It was a fifty-fifty chance she went north. I jerked the steering wheel to the right, and hit the gas.

Weaving through traffic, I kept my eyes peeled for her carriage, but to no avail. After a few miles or so, I gave up. "Just my luck, wouldn't you know it," I said to myself and drove back downtown.

A hundred questions raced through my mind before I found a parking space on Canal Street and trudged across the bridge toward Boots' joint. *Is she in with Boots?* If so, I was the world's biggest chump. From every angle, Teri appeared to be knee deep in this mess. Somebody must have pinned a sign on my back that read *sucker*, because everybody was playing me for a sap.

By the time I legged into Roscoe's cool, dark interior, I was steamed. The bartender was polishing the bar, getting ready for the night's trade when I stomped leather and entered the hallway to Boots' office. Without knocking, I opened the door and walked in. Sam and Tom had their guns drawn and pointed at me before I made a second step.

"Easy boys."

The duo obeyed their boss and put their guns away while I gingerly set my gun down on the small table off to the side. Sam sat down and casually took out his blade, but Tom remained standing, watching me like a hawk.

"What the hell, Verriet, didn't anybody ever teach you any manners? Don't you know better than to come busting in here?" Boots said angrily.

"Aw, dry up! What was Teri Marcus doing here?"

At my outburst, Tom came up on my left side and Sam braced me on the right.

"Pipe down, Verriet, or I'm going to have you thrown out."

"Dammit, answer my question. What was she doing here?"

"If you gotta know, she came to pick up money I owed Joe."

"You expect me to believe that?" I asked hotly.

"I don't give a shit whether you believe it or not, it's the truth. She said she was goin' on a trip and needed the dough."

What he said made sense, but I hated to admit it. She was taking it on the lam.

"Did you know Chuck was iced at her place a few hours ago?"

It was Boots' turn to be surprised. "Chuck—you mean our sax player?"

"Bingo," I said smugly. "Somebody put a pill in his skull."

"The cops know about it?"

"Oh, yeah, and you can guess who they're looking to question."

"They think Mrs. Marcus did it?"

"As someone told me recently, it's not who I think did it that's important, it's who the D.A. thinks did it. And I've got more good news for you, Chuck tore Marcus' house apart before he was popped. The cops know Chuck was an addict and they're raising a lot of questions about you."

Boots' face turned red, his breathing became labored and tiny sweat beads formed on his forehead. He looked like he was about to have a heart attack.

"Me! What the hell do the cops want with me?" he shouted. "So the guy was a hop head. I was his employer, not his supplier. What the hell did you tell them, Verriet?" he asked as a line of drool rolled over his thick lower lip and down his chin.

"Hey, I didn't say shit. I barely got out of there with my skin intact. The D.A. is pouring on the heat because election time is getting close. If the cops don't find who murdered Joe and Chuck soon, the D.A.'s gonna run his finger down his who's-been-naughty list and pick somebody to tumble."

I didn't need to mention that his name was closer to the top than mine. *This cracker box is set to blow sky high, and when it does, there's a slight chance I'll make it out alive and out of the gendarme's search light.*

Boots stared at me without blinking. His cogitative wheels were turning like a printing press. If my guess was right, he was sizing me up for the job of fall guy to take the heat off.

"Don't even think about it, Boots. The cops know Chuck worked for you and they know he was looking for something he knew you lost. If I were you, I'd account for a missing article and fast, like a duplicate set of books—anything to throw the cops off the trail."

He considered my statement, and glanced up at Tom and Sam. "Somebody's been talkin'," he barked to the pair. "Find out who and what they've been saying. Check on everybody, and I do mean everybody. And do it fast," he ordered.

After his boys hauled bunions, Boots redirected his attention back to me. "Time's running out, Verriet. You better come through with the goods. Pronto. Otherwise, I figure the cops are gonna put the finger on you and Mrs. Marcus for both kills."

"Not if I can point them in another direction first."

"You point 'em my way, and I'll have the boys take you fishing in Lake Michigan."

Why not? Everybody else is using me for bait.

Chapter Twenty-five

As usual, Bobby was working on some scores when I approached him. "Bobby, I've got some more bad news for you."

He groaned loudly. "We're fired?"

"No, the band isn't fired. Chuck's dead."

He frowned, sadly nodding his head from side to side. "I'm not surprised. Sooner or later his habit was bound to catch up with him."

"His habit didn't kill him. He was murdered. Somebody filled his noggin with lead."

"Who'd shoot the kid?"

"Somebody wrapped up in Joe's killing. He was killed in Joe's house."

"Dammit. First Joe, and now, Chuck. What the hell's going on, Nick?"

"I wish to hell I knew, Bobby. It's a mess and I have the feeling it's going to get a lot messier before it gets better. Remember what I said before?"

"Yeah, look for another job, right?"

"Uh-huh. It goes double now."

"What about you? Why don't we team up and have our own band? You do arrangements and bookings and I'll handle personnel. That way we cut out the middle man."

"I'm flattered. I'll think about it, Bobby, but right now I'm knee deep, and the shit's pouring in faster than I can shovel it out. Which reminds me, did you see Teri earlier?"

"Yeah, but she didn't stop and talk. She went straight to Boots' office without so much as a howdy-do. Came out five minutes later and left."

"Did she ever come here to hear you guys play?"

"Naw, she'd stop in once in a while when we was rehearsin', and ask Joe for some money or somethin', but she never stuck around."

"She ever talk to the band members?"

"She'd say 'hi,' but that was about all."

"How about Chuck? She ever talk to him?"

"Man, what you gettin' at?"

"Teri called me from her abode about thirty minutes before I found Chuck. I think she's skipped town. She wasn't home when I got there and she beat a hot trail here immediately afterward to collect Joe's back pay."

"What?" he asked in shock.

"Yeah, Chuck tore the place apart looking for something and it looks like Teri may have breezed him. Did Joe ever confiscate Chuck's supply, or anyone else's?"

"Chuck's the only one who rode the horse besides Honey. When Joe found her supply, he tossed it and fired her."

"Do me a favor, will you?"

"Sure, Nick."

"Keep your eyes open. I'd like to know who sees Boots and when his two thugs, Tom and Sam, come and go. Don't go out of your way and don't let them know you're watching, though. Alright?"

"No problem. I been playin' clubs so long, watchin' my back's a habit—self-preservation if you know what I mean," he said wryly.

I considered asking him to keep a special eye out for Teri, but thought better of it. Chances were she was long gone, and if he did see her, I had serious doubts she'd stick around to see me. *She's gone and in more ways than one.* The thought made the old yearning surface. With a concerted effort I fought down the urge and focused on the present situation.

"You gonna play with us again, Nick? We can sure use you," Bobby inquired in a pleading voice.

It was against my better judgment, but one look at his troubled countenance and I capitulated. "I'll try, Bobby."

With a look of relief, he said, "Thanks, man. The joint's closed tomorrow and we'll see what Tuesday brings, huh?"

I nodded and left without telling him that I had a premonition tonight would be the last time I played anywhere ever again except in prison.

The afternoon sun shone brightly when I stepped outside and it took my eyes a moment to adjust to the light. My car's seats were blazing hot. I reached behind the passenger seat, grabbed a towel and draped it over the driver's seat for relief. When I turned my head, a two-tone Sunbeam Super Sport caught my eye, a sleek job driven by a tough looking colored guy wearing all black. He gave me a casual look as I eased my heap out of its parking space. I reached the stoplight on the corner, looked in the rearview mirror, and saw him pull out and begin to follow me.

"Ducky, just ducky," I exclaimed aloud. It was the icing on the cake. Now the coloreds must have decided to take an active hand in the affair. As if I didn't have enough to worry about. I was fed up with everybody following me around town. It was time to put my lizzy through its paces. At the next intersection, I took a right and hit the gas. When I came to an alleyway, I jerked the wheel to the left and kicked the kidneys out of my carburetor to the opposite end. Barely bothering to slowdown, I swung onto the next street and made a right. Burning five bucks of rubber off my treads, I throttled every ounce of energy out of my flivver.

Without looking to see if my tail was still behind me, I turned into another alley. The path was partially blocked by a trash bin. I coaxed my flivver toward the bin, giving it a good kiss and sending it caroming off a brick building and into the middle of the alleyway before I drove straight for two more blocks, and turned left. After weaving in and out of a couple more alleys and driving completely around the last block, I went west for two blocks and parked. Five minutes elapsed and the Sunbeam didn't show, so I beat a hasty retreat to my apartment.

My shirt was soaked with sweat when I climbed out of my car. Safely ensconced in my apartment, I chipped off some ice and made myself a tall, cool drink, and took it with me to the bathroom. After a quick shower and change of clothes, I settled back on my sofa after tuning in a ball game on my Philco. The Cubs were playing, and soon the rhythmic sing-song of the play-by-play announcer lulled me to sleep.

Fans were cheering somebody's home run when I woke up in a daze. Then it hit me. A piece of puzzle fell into place. I remembered when Gale first came into my office with a case—an instrument case. At the time, I recalled thinking the case was for a tenor saxophone. It must have been Chuck's.

I grabbed my phone, and told the operator to connect me to Roscoe's. A few seconds later, somebody picked up the phone and I asked for Bobby. When he came on the line, I said, "Bobby, this is Nick. I've got a quick question for you. Did Chuck leave his horn case lying around?"

He told me to wait while he went to take a look. A couple of minutes later he returned on the line and announced, "No."

"Can you tell me what his case looked like?"

"It's an old black leather job beat to hell."

"Yeah, sounds right. Thanks Bobby. See you later," I said and hung-up.

It was nearing seven, time to head over to Gale's. With trepidation, I drove to her apartment. There were some questions I had to ask her. An overwhelming feeling of helplessness overcame me. Everyone involved in the case seemed to be slipping away from me, melting into nothingness like a shooting star. Unfortunately, time was carrying my future away, too, as it disintegrated into the sandy scape of my existence.

I strode up the stairs to Gale's apartment. A pleasant aroma tickled my olfactory senses. I knocked on her door and she shouted for me to come in. If the meal tasted half as good as it smelled I was in for a real treat. The last home cooked dinner I had was the one with Teri at the cabin, and it hardly qualified.

Gale came out of the kitchen wearing an apron over a loose fitting pair of slacks and a light pink silk blouse. She blew a wisp of hair off her forehead, came over and gave me a lingering kiss.

"Perfect timing, I just took the roast out of the oven."

"I picked up a bottle of red from an Italian guy who smuggles the stuff in. Would you like a glass?"

"Sure," she replied, "sounds great."

"I could smell the roast outside on the landing. I'm surprised you don't have the neighbors beating down your door to join us for dinner."

"You sure have a knack for always saying the right things at the right time?"

I wish Teri felt the same way!

"I only wish I had a knack for *doing* the right things at the right time."

"Hmm, timing is everything, isn't it?" she ruminated.

"Don't I know it. You can make more money, more friends, more of anything, but you can't make more time. And my time is running out."

"That bad, Nick?" she asked in a consoling voice.

"Yeah, but let's have dinner. I'm starved. We can discuss things afterward."

We took our wine into the small dining area off the kitchen. She insisted on me sitting at the table while she served up the meal. We began with a dinner salad accompanied by a loaf of fresh baked bread. The pot roast followed, prepared the way I like it, with lots of onions, carrots, and potatoes. The meat was so tender it melted in my mouth. When we finished, Gale brought out a cherry pie for dessert.

Afterward, we adjourned to her living room with cups of strong coffee. I eased back on the sofa feeling full and content. We enjoyed another brew while Gale threw on a couple of records by Bessie Smith, her favorite blues singer.

Dinner had been so pleasant, I decided not to tell her about Chuck. I wanted the evening to end on a good note. There were a few angles for me yet to explore and time was of the essence, as the attorneys say, but I selfishly seized this one small respite, away from the ugliness of the case. *After all, this might be the last good, carefree time I experience in a long time.* Little did I know how right I was.

Chapter Twenty-six

Monday

Gale and I managed an early start to the day, joined by the morning rush crowd for breakfast at the same neighborhood eatery we had patronized yesterday morning. Our waitress gave us a knowing look and said something under her breath to one of the other gals before motioning in our direction.

The sky was gray with rain in the forecast. Over a couple orders of French toast, I began thinking about Gale in a new light. She interrupted my thought processes by saying, "Nick, where are you this morning? You seem preoccupied."

"Yeah. Last night was special, Gale. One of the nicest evenings I've had in a very long time."

She frowned. "You seem almost maudlin about it."

"You don't understand."

"You're right, I don't. So tell me," she said beseechingly.

"When I was a kid, I loved the old detective stories. I used to hunt out all the old Nick Carter stories and anything else I could find and stay up late reading them. Those stories were the big reason I decided to become a private detective. But I was young and foolish. The business isn't anything like in those stories. Being clever or a tough dick gets you nowhere, except to an early grave. There's too much political corruption and the mob's too entrenched. All this job does is strip me of all my illusions—and very few of them survived the war. After last night, it makes me think I should quit."

"So why don't you?"

"I can't unless the cops solve the murders, and that's as likely as me becoming the next mayor."

"Murders? Who else was murdered?" she asked nervously.

"Chuck was murdered yesterday in Joe's house. That's where I spent the better part of the day."

"Chuck? Murdered?" she asked with a stunned expression.

"Yeah, a lead pill to the back of the head doesn't leave much doubt."

"What was he doing at Joe's house?"

"Looking for the same thing I am. It's not money is it, Gale? It's drugs, isn't it?"

Tears welled in her orbs and spilled down her cheeks. I signaled the waitress for the check. When she brought it over, I stuffed a deuce in her hand, and told her to keep the change.

"C'mon, let's get out of here and go someplace where we can talk."

Gale silently nodded and we left the restaurant. It was raining, so we sprinted to her apartment and she put the coffee pot on. I sat quietly in the living room listening to the steady drone of raindrops against the front windowpane until she joined me on the couch, handing me a steaming cup of coffee.

"Why did you tell me Boots was missing money?"

She looked up, a defiant gleam in her eyes, "Isn't he?"

"I don't think so. What makes you so sure?"

"I overheard Boots talking about it."

"Tell me exactly what you overheard."

She sat up, arched her back, and replied, "One afternoon I went to Boots' office to ask him if I could switch days off. I wanted to see *No, No, Nanette* before it left town. His office door was closed, but I heard him yelling. He mentioned a suitcase of money and said someone never showed up with it. He threatened to have somebody killed if he didn't get his money. I hurried away from his door and hung around the bar area to see who came out of his office, but nobody did. I guess he must have been talking on the telephone."

I switched subjects again to keep her off-guard. "How did Chuck happen to come here?"

With a slight squint, she said, "Joe lost his tenor player. Boots must have called Chuck."

"Did you know Chuck well in Detroit?"

"So-so. He was a nice kid back then. For some reason he used to confide in me. He told me about his upbringing—broken family, alcoholic mother, the whole spiel. I sympathized with him since my story was similar. I felt sorry for him—I used to bring him home once in a while to make sure he got a good meal."

"Was he a drug user then?"

"Not at first," she said, pressing her scrumptious curves into me on the sofa, curling one leg under her. "I mean, not when I first knew him. He got hooked after he started making a name for himself. He began to hang out with a couple of well-known jazzmen who were users, and I think he wanted to be like them."

"What about after he came to Chicago?"

"By then he was different, Nick. He was hooked and there wasn't anything I could do for him. I wanted to help him, but all he wanted was money for junk and I wasn't about to give him any. He'd talk to me when he was evened-out, like old times, but mostly he was out looking for his next score or money to buy more junk."

"Do you remember when you first came to my office?"

She chuckled, "Yeah, I thought you were a weirdo or something."

"You had a tenor sax case with you. It was Chuck's. How was it you had his case?"

"I forgot about that," she said with a small smile. "Boots' boys had been following me and I wanted to throw them for a loop, so I grabbed the first thing I could find which would pass for a case of sorts. Sort of stupid, wasn't it?"

Ignoring her question, I asked, "Didn't you think Boots would get mad if he found out about you hiring me to find his stolen dough?"

"Sure, but what could he do about it? It's all hot money," she replied tartly.

"He could fire you if he doesn't kill you," I snapped back.

"He threatened to fire me when he found out I was in your office, but I told him I hired you to find the pawn shop where Chuck had hocked his horn so I could get it back for him."

"And he bought that?"

"Sure? I can be very convincing when I want to be."

"Yeah, I believe you."

"Believe it or not, Chuck *had* hocked his horn for a dose; he was always doing that."

Her tale was a little too pat, but I let it go. She looked at me as if she was suddenly sizing me up to see if I bought her story. The creeping willies scaled my spine as I thought about Chuck lying on the floor in Joe and Teri's bedroom.

What added to my sense of disequilibrium was the fact Gale didn't seem particularly saddened by either Joe or Chuck's death. *Is she that hardened to the breaks, the unforgiving side of life? Is she inexplicably involved in either of their murders? If so, I'm with her now, and where does that leave me?*

Chapter Twenty-seven

Before I departed, I told Gale I'd be too busy to see her until the following night at the club. She accepted my news with a shrug and told me to be careful.

I drove straight to St. Anthony's, circumvented visitor sign-in, and took the staircase up to the fourth floor. Checking that none of the hospital staff, especially the nurses I had spoken to earlier, were around, I sauntered to Butters' room, and took a quick peek around the door.

Butters looked like hell. His bruises were peaking like trees in autumn. His chest barely moved with each shallow breath. I thought he was sleeping, but he opened one of his swollen eyelids when I put my hand on his shoulder. He gave me a crooked smile and murmured something unintelligible.

"Looks like you're going to make it buddy," I said inanely.

"Yaw," he replied weakly.

"Man, I'm sorrier than I can say for bringing you into this mess. I'll do whatever I can to see you back on your feet, Butters. Count on it, buddy."

He motioned with his finger for me to come closer. Cocking my head to one side, I leaned over his bed and he rasped, "Get da bastards for me," in a hoarse whisper.

"You bet, buddy," I assured him contritely. "Who did it?"

Tapping into what little inner strength he possessed, Butters leaned forward and whispered, "Rupert's 33 Club," before he collapsed back on the bed.

"Who were you asking about?"

His barely opened eyelid fluttered. "Him," he replied in a faint voice that faded away before he nodded off.

The rain had increased to a drenching downpour as I ran to my car. Safely ensconced inside, I sat and listened to the rain pummel the roof. *Who was Butters referring to when he said, 'him'? Boots? A visit to the 33 Club tonight might provide some answers.*

I wheeled my chariot to the cleaners to pick up my laundry. During the drive, an idea began to coalesce as I rearranged the order of events from the time I discovered Joe's body to the present. I tried to force the solution to the puzzle into my consciousness, but it was the wrong approach. I had to allow my brain to sort through all the data and come up with the answers in its own good time. Experience had taught me the best thing to do was to get a good night's sleep. Then maybe it would come to me.

After a quick stop at the cleaners, I headed straight for my apartment. As I waited on the garage ramp for the electric door to open, I turned on my car's lights, the dark rainy skies making it difficult to see into the garage against the contrasting grey cement. I pressed the door switch, slowly wheeled my buggy down the entrance ramp, and turned left. That's when I spotted wet footsteps trailing off down the length of the garage from someone who had walked in from the outside earlier. Someone would have had to wait in the rain to enter the garage through the automobile entrance rather than enter the main building and take the elevator down. *That doesn't make sense.*

I yanked out my roscoe and slammed the gearshift into low, slowly driving toward my parking space. The garage spanned the entire length of the three buildings it serviced, over a hundred yards long. At the juncture of each building, concrete walls jutted out, roughly fifteen feet from both sides.

I had the advantage of being on guard since the earlier attempt on my life. If it was the same gunner, he'd know just where I parked and how to arrange the perfect place to pick me off. Looking from side to side, I eased the car up to the first of the walls. All clear. But no sooner had I passed by the dividers, than a head peered around the next set of walls on the right.

Without hesitation, I doused my flivver's light, threw the gearshift into reverse, and mashed my foot on the accelerator. My rust bucket screamed in protest and nearly drowned out the sounds of the gunfire. I immediately scrunched down. Flames erupted from around both sides of the concrete walls. Dull thuds smacked as bullets kissed my car. I jerked the wheel and gunned my flivver backwards up the ramp towards the garage door. With a sharp screech, I braked and without putting the car in park, I opened my door and dove out to the safety of the walls between the first and second building.

The incline where I had left my jalopy caused it to roll forward. An unintended circumstance that worked to my favor because both shooters stepped out from their ambush spots and fired repeated volleys at my chariot as it rolled toward them. I knelt down, took careful aim and shot the bastard on my left. He went down with a scream. Shifting my aim to his cohort, my shot went wide and chipped a small piece of cement off the wall by his head.

I let loose two more shots as he legged it over to his wounded partner and pulled him to safety. The next move was theirs and I didn't have long to wait. Seconds later, a motor fired to life, and a black and maroon Lincoln Phaeton pulled out of a parking spot about twenty feet further from where the duo had taken up their firing positions. I ducked behind the wall as the car sped toward me. When it drew abreast of my position, the driver's gun barked a final shot in my general direction. The slug missed me by a few feet. I stepped around the nearest car and repaid the favor, the rear glass shattering before they reached the ramp.

The driver jumped out to hit the garage door switch. Knowing it takes a bit of time for the large door to open fully once triggered, I hauled bunions after them. Their car in my gunsight, I emptied my gat's clip. The moment the garage door fully opened, the driver punched the octane and ruby-red taillights disappeared as they made their getaway.

With a string of invectives a mile long, I examined the damage to my car. Two bullets had pierced the rear window and another had hit the rear end. The side had four bullet holes dotting its length, but as luck would have it, none of the bullets had penetrated the engine compartment. The front bumper, dented where it had rolled down the ramp and hit the far wall, now matched its rear counterpart. With the previous damage to my car and today's holes and dents, my insurance company was going to be more than a little skeptical about any explanation I might dream up to account for the damage. On the other hand, there had been so many mob shootings in the city of late, I might get away with telling them my car was unfortunately parked where one of the mob's torpedos opened up with a Chicago typewriter.

Somebody was going to pay and I knew where to start collecting. By the dim light from the naked bulbs lining the garage ceiling, I had recognized the driver—the short stocky hood who worked for Al Hewitt.

I drove my car into my parking spot and walked back with my flashlight to where the shooters had taken up their stations. Getting down on all fours, I searched under all the cars parked in the general area until I felt reasonably assured I had located all the spent shell casings. Half were from a .38 caliber and the others from a .22. Luckily, nobody was around again to call the cops since everyone who lived in the building was a member of the working class. *Me, too,* I reminded myself. *I'm just a working stiff-to-be.*

The car Al's two henchmen drove didn't match either of the cars that tailed me before. *How many damn people are in on this thing? And neither of Al's goons fit the physical make-up of the first guy who tried to ambush me in the garage. At least I hit one of the henchmen.* Unfortunately, there seemed to be more than enough goons ready to take his place.

Chapter Twenty-eight

Enough was enough. It was time to extricate myself from the middle of this Gordian knot. First, I had to do something about my ride. Besides being banged-up and riddled with bullets, too many guys out for my red corpuscles knew my beater's profile.

I drove to Louie's garage. Louie, the owner and head mechanic, was the best. He knew every make and model down to the minutest part. He took one look at my wheels, and with a shake of his head, asked, "Are those what I think they are?" as he appraised the bullet holes.

"Yeah, but don't tell anybody, okay, Louie?"

"Uh, I dunno, Nick. I don't need no cops comin' round. You in some kind of trouble or somethin'?"

"Yeah, but not what you're thinking. I promise no recriminations will befall you for fixing my car."

"Huh?" Louie replied with a puzzled look.

I worked away at him another ten minutes. He eventually saw things my way after I told him I'd pay time-and-a-half for the job. The extra cabbage placated him, and he asked me to help him cover my car with a tarp before I left.

"How long before it's fixed?" I asked hopefully as I tucked my corner of the tarp around a fender.

"Depends how fast I get parts. What color you want it repainted when I'm done with the body work?"

"Same color," I answered, then quickly amended, "No, Louie, paint it maroon."

He nodded agreement and informed me, "I'm pretty back-logged, Nick, but I'll try to give it some time after hours. Seems like everybody and their uncle is getting their cars shot up by these mobsters."

I asked again. "How long will it take?"

"Dunno, could be a week, could be a month," he replied noncommittedly.

Deep down I had a suspicion Louie was making excuses for not working on my car during regular hours—when someone might

138

question the bullet holes. Beggars can't be choosers, so I told him that would be fine.

"You got anything around here I can drive till my car is ready?"

"You're in luck. One of Capone's gang dropped off that Chevrolet in the corner a couple of weeks ago. The cops pinched the owner for a holdup and he's cooling his heels in stir. He won't be needing it for a while I reckon."

It was a cheap, nondescript black 490 model, but as I said before about beggars, I graciously accepted Louie's offer.

"One thing, though, Nick, I ain't responsible for any problems with it. Bring it back in good shape or I'll have to report it stolen. I'm not going to tell anybody I loaned it to ya, especially if it gets shot up."

I assured him I'd take good care of the heap before I climbed in, heeled the starter and backed out of the garage.

Outside Boots' office, I prepared for a confrontation and easily assumed a countenance of extreme displeasure. Flinging open the door brought Tom and Sam to immediate attention. They relaxed when they glimmed me as the intruder. I gingerly handed Tom my gun, grabbed a chair, and plunked my carcass down as if I owned the place.

"You owe me a lot of money, Boots."

"How do you figure?"

"My car's in the garage, shot to hell."

Boots adjusted himself in his chair and leaned forward, placing his elbows on his desk. "What happened?"

I gave him a quick recap of events. When the moment was ripe, I casually added, "They were Al Hewitt's boys."

He reacted as if I had shot him instead of one of Hewitt's thugs. His face twisted into any ugly mask and the muscle below his right eye began to twitch. He fought for control as he sat there blubbering, his mouth working overtime. He wiped his mouth with the back of his hand.

When he regained a modicum of composure, he asked, "Are you sure they were Hewitt's boys?"

"Absolutely. They were the same goons tending door when I talked to Al. I winged the big one. The small, stout bastard was the driver. If you don't believe me have a look at my car."

"Son-of-a-bitch. That bastard's makin' a play," he shouted to Tom and Sam. "Why didn't you find out about him?" he asked with a nasty, accusing gleam in his eye.

Sam stuttered, "B-b-but we did check, b-boss. Everything came out all right. Al said we was all good as far as he was concerned."

"And you bright boys believed him, huh?" he sneered.

"Honest boss, Al said things were copacetic," echoed Tom.

Boots shifted his gaze back to me. "I'll have the boys check into this. If you're feedin' me a line of shit Verriet, I'm going to cut you up into little pieces and use you for chum."

I shrugged. "Check all you want. Now what about my car?"

He narrowed his eyes and growled, "I'll pay for your damn car, now get the hell out of here."

"How 'bout some fixit money before I go?" I asked boldly. He surprised me by opening his wallet and shelling out copious cabbage. Without a word, I scooped up the green and left. *That ought to stir things up.* Now it was time to wait and see what shit hit the fan.

I was long overdue at my office for no other reason than to pick up messages. There was always a remote chance Teri had called, or a new client wanted to contract my services. The skies had turned a darker gray and it looked like the city was in for a real downpour as I drove towards the lake.

My prophecy came true as the skies opened wide, emptying buckets by the time I reached State Street. I recently read an article about a guy filing for a patent for windscreen wipers for cars. I was all for the idea as I fought a losing battle to see through the deluge. Slowing to a crawl and occasionally sticking my head out the side window, I circled around the block in search of a parking space. After my third failed attempt, I said the hell with it, and parked in the alleyway.

Dashing through the back door of my office building, I stamped my feet on an entrance mat and removed my hat. My sodden shoes squeaked with each step I took toward the elevator.

My office was as I had last left it. A small pile of mail, highlighted by a couple of message slips, lay on the floor near the mail slot. I extracted the messages and read them. They were both from Teri. She had left only her name, no message or number where I could call her back. She had my home number, but maybe she felt it safer to call me at the office.

Should I wait in the office for her to call again? The police knew of our relationship and maybe she figured they had a stakeout on my apartment. She couldn't know my office phone was being tapped. Hell, maybe my home phone was tapped, too.

I decided to kill some time in the office with hopes we'd match up. My coffee pot gurgled away as I spread out the rain-soaked evening edition of the *Times* across my desktop.

Big bold letters announced a large mob shootout between Capone's gang and a rival faction that didn't like Capone taking over as boss from Torrio who had decided to retire when he found a diet of lead didn't agree with him. The details were horrifying—three guys dead and two more wounded at the scene. The scanty facts, preliminarily disclosed by the police commissioner, were skewed in Capone's favor. What sent the newsboys scrambling was the fact that among the innocent bystanders wounded was a pregnant woman and her two year old daughter. The reporter alluded to society's increasing insensitivity to murder—how mob shootings had become nearly commonplace in the city.

All the attention the sensational case was receiving was sure to preoccupy the D.A.—meaning I could breathe a little easier for the time being. The timing of the case couldn't have been better from the D.A.'s viewpoint, practically made to order for front-page publicity to carry him to election time. Knowing corruption ran from the rank-and-file up through to the mayor's office, I wondered if the D.A. had a finger in the trouble. When crime reached a standstill, maybe he decided to stir the pot, go for the big print. If not, it was a helluva coincidence.

When I finished reading the article, I felt sickened as I sat back in my office chair and thought about all those poor, innocent victims falling prey to the gangsters. At least the police had caught the two wounded bastards. I only hoped some slick shyster didn't prevent them from getting their due.

I flicked on my office radio and tuned in to a local news station. Sitting back in my chair with my third cup of java, I listened to a reporter's on-the-scene account of the shooting. The police had cordoned off the area and stationed a twenty-four hour guard to ward off nosy neighbors and the usual plethora of miscreants sensational crimes always attracted. Continuous talk of the mob's control of the politicians, interspersed with the occasional comments of the authorities and legal bigwigs, consumed most of the news report. It was the usual dribble with neighbors reporting what a nice man one of the dead killers had been and how shocked they were when they learned the ghastly truth about him.

A brief interlude followed for the latest sports and weather reports before a local business summary concluded the remaining city news. Finally, in passing, the station's news announcer concluded the program reporting how two bodies had been discovered in an old abandoned warehouse on the near southwest side. I nearly missed the report until the broadcaster said the police connected the two men with the numbers rackets.

I immediately grabbed the phone on my desk and dialed Powers' number. He wasn't available so I dialed the number for Ray Stepson.

He answered, and after I identified myself, he said, "Thought I'd hear from you," with a chuckle. "What do you know about Erickson and Dubrovich?"

"Who?"

"Al Hewitt's boys," he replied.

"Oh, I didn't know their names." I debated whether to tell him about the shoot-out in the garage and decided to wait for the time being. "The last time I lamped Al's gazabos was when I visited his place of business. You might remember, I told you about it. What about Al?" I hurriedly asked to redirect his focus.

"What about him?" he asked suspiciously.

"How did he make out?" I prompted.

"I wouldn't know. We can't locate him. Either he's in hiding, or we haven't found his body yet," Ray replied matter-of-factly.

"Maybe the former racket boys are setting up a squeeze play to recover their former territories."

"We already considered that angle. You got anything else to add?"

"How were they killed, the newscast didn't say?" I asked in return to his question.

"This is just between us, Verriet. We're not letting out details yet, understand?"

"Absolutely," I affirmed.

"Both were shot gang style with .38s." Before I could comment and steer the conversation elsewhere, he asked, "What caliber gun do you use?"

It was useless to lie since Powers knew I sported a .45. "I carry a .45. Why do you ask?"

"Damned peculiar, Erickson was shot in the shoulder, too. The attending physician thinks it was from a .45."

He left the information hanging out there, waiting for me to pick up the ball. "That's out of left field, alright," I agreed. "38's . . . hmm . . . sounds like Boots might be involved," I suggested to divert the conversation.

"Verriet, I think you know a lot more than you're saying."

"No, just thinking out loud, Ray. I've only guesses at this point, the same ones we discussed in Powers' office. So what's next?" I asked not expecting him to tell me anything useful.

I was right. He answered, "Nothin'. I'm going to sit tight and see what Boots' next move is, and you're going to keep me informed of anything I should know."

"Of course, Ray," I said playing along. "If I was you, I'd keep an eye out for more trouble, though. If Al made a play, the other bosses might be getting ideas, too," I said and hung up.

Ray was trying to put the squeeze on me, but it wasn't going to work. The bullet I had shot Erickson with went clean through him. I knew because I pried it out of the cement wall of my garage, and it was now resting comfortably in my pocket alongside the other spent cartridges I'd collected.

Chapter Twenty-nine

I fell asleep in my chair and awoke with a start. Thoughts were racing through my mind and suddenly a gear dropped into place. "I'll be damned," I said aloud as the realization surfaced from my subconscious, breaking through the muddy waters to rattle my cogitative wheelworks.

Just like that, I knew why Boots was taking over the numbers racket. More importantly, I knew why he kept the former runners and bosses in place. Working the numbers was just a smoke screen. What he was after was the network. As vice goes, the numbers racket was low on the police totem pole—especially since Prohibition gave them so much to work on, not to mention the publicity. Nobody got hurt playing numbers for the most part, except for the poor suckers hooked on gambling money they couldn't afford to lose.

Boots was smart, but I had underestimated him. Behind his well-appointed frills and dressings lurked a mobster with inspiration. He knew Prohibition was his best friend—it took the heat off the other vice areas, like numbers, and anyone connected with them. Capone and his crew had captured the public's imagination and the D.A. knew it so he concentrated all the manpower available to go after the bootleggers. The time was ripe for somebody to step in and consolidate the numbers game and Boots figured he was the chosen.

The numbers racket ran smoothly, except for the occasional heist by some naïve gunsel. Nobody in their right mind robbed the bagmen. It was a well-known fact that to rob one of the carriers was tantamount to writing your own death warrant. The mob boys in charge let the repercussions be known in no uncertain terms by setting some very gruesome examples of gangster justice whenever robbers were caught.

Boots knew the numbers game in Detroit and that knowledge quickly paid off when he thought up his brilliant scheme. With a well-oiled numbers network, he could control traffic in both directions, to and from the individual district bosses. And what was better, the money made from the numbers paid for everyone involved. Once he had control of the numbers downtown and to the west and southern reaches, he had everything in place to run dope.

Boots was going to make himself king of the dope world. Everything was in place except one necessity—the drug supply. Chuck and Honey's connections probably supplied part of the answer for him to sew up the drugs into and out of the city. His boys followed the leads they provided to their source. One thing would lead to another and before much time passed, Boots would have the main sources identified and impress upon them that he was open for business and in charge.

How far along his planning had progressed is the big question. If my thinking is right, he has everything in place and is ready to make the first big purchase. Either that or he already made the purchase when his machinery went haywire. Somebody figured out what he was up to and stole the goods, either money or dope. That somebody must have been Joe and he wasn't talking.

I was sure I was on the right track, but a couple of major puzzle pieces remained. *First, what was stolen—money or drugs, or both? Second, why did Joe steal from Boots when he had to know Boots would have him killed? Third, did anyone else figure out Boots' scheme?* Word traveled fast in the underworld. It would be mighty hard to keep a secret like Boots' from leaking. Tom and Sam knew how to keep their mouths shut, but Boots had set all the numbers' bosses thinking when he kept them at their old jobs. Eventually someone would get wise and spill the beans.

What would happen after that was anybody's guess. Boots probably figured the risk was worth the rewards. Look at the money pouring through Capone's operation. The biggest difference between the two was that Capone had the general populace on his side. Everybody and his or her uncle, except for the occasional Aunt Minny, took a nip now and then, but opiate use was a horse of a different color.

Being the bright boy that he was, Boots had an answer for that, too. He kept the old bosses in place. If the cops tracked down the channels of distribution, the first place they'd come to would be the numbers stations. Boots would follow Capone's example and have a bevy of shyster lawyers at his bidding to extricate any of his gang's members from the clutches of the legal system in no time flat. Yeah, I had to hand it to him; Boots was an opportunist with a vision.

Nevertheless, Boots was relatively new in town. One area of major concern to him had to be the old bosses. Even if they hadn't figured out the drug angle, they weren't accustomed to taking orders from anybody. Resentment would undoubtedly build over time, and that went double once Boots' operation went into overdrive. Whoever came up with the old adage of hell hath no fury like that of a woman scorned never mingled with mobsters. I never knew one of them who wouldn't slit his brother's throat if he discovered his sibling was raking dough off the top at their expense.

There was one way to find out what was brewing amongst the bosses and that was to follow up where Butters had left off. Time for me to make a trip to Cicero.

Chapter Thirty

The 33 Club was on the ground floor of the middle of three identical four-story gray office buildings. The parking lot was dotted by cars scattered at irregular intervals—a mix of late workers and early club revelers. Muted music drifted out into the cavernous hallway when I entered the building. Heavy mahogany doors with large brass numbers announced the club's entrance, and a hard-boy decked out in soup and fish greeted me inside the door. The evening's featured singer was belting out *Ain't We Got Fun* to the house band's accompaniment.

I settled on a stool at the center bar. The guy singing was good and the band was spot on. I sat and listened to the music and wondered why mobsters were attracted to the entertainment business. Easy answer: there was money in it. *How else could they move their illegal hooch?* After downing a near beer, I ordered another. When the bartender pushed my drink in front of me, I slid a fin across the bar toward him.

"Were you working Saturday night?"

"Yep," he replied laconically as he rang up my order and deposited two-bits in the till. He counted out my change in front of me. I pushed it back toward him. "Do you remember a guy here Saturday, male-pattern bald with long brown hair, slight build, about five feet ten?"

"Doesn't ring a bell," he said and left my money on the bar as he went to wait on another patron.

I gulped my beer and watched the bartender. One thing about near beer was the fact you could drink the swill all night without getting drunk. When he returned to ask me if I wanted a refill, I said, "Yeah, another suds, and one more question." He looked at me with a bored expression. "You couldn't miss this guy I'm talking about, he has funny ears. They stick out at forty-five degree angles from his head. Ring any bells now?"

The bartender nodded and said, "Yeah, I remember now. He asked me if we had any anisette. First time anybody ever asked me for that sticky sweet stuff."

"Damn, I should have remembered that," I said aloud, scolding myself. "Do you remember anyone with him?" I asked hopefully.

"Yeah, he was talking to Jimmy, one of the regulars."

"Is Jimmy here now?"

He gave me a dubious look. "What's with the twenty questions, fella?"

"It's a game I like playing," I replied and extracted another fin from my wallet. I added it to the bills on the bar and pushed them toward him. "The guy with the ears is a good friend of mine. Somebody beat the shit out of him Saturday night and I'm trying to catch whoever did it. I'm a private dick," I added and flashed him my license.

He frowned and said, "He's not here, but he usually comes in around eleven." He put the money for my beer in the register and palmed the rest—a practiced move—one he probably performed a dozen times a night.

Going on eleven o'clock, I nursed my beer and waited. About a quarter after, I heard the bartender greet a tall lanky red-haired guy in his early thirties, "The usual, Jimmy?" in a voice louder than necessary.

That was my cue. Jimmy seated himself a couple of stools away from me on my left. I signaled for another beer, and when the bartender served it up, I handed him another fin and told him to keep the change as a way to acknowledge his tip-off. Half-way through my beer, an attractive brunette approached me and asked if I wanted to dance.

"I'm flattered doll. Maybe later, huh?"

"You had your chance, Ace," she said huffily and moved on.

You can't win 'em all, I thought and glanced over at Red.

He was wearing a dark blue silk sport coat with a white cotton shirt and a red striped tie. He was in shape, probably did some sparring at a local gym. Every so often, he and the bartender would have a little chat, and each time I kept my fingers crossed the bartender wouldn't tell Jimmy about me. But the bartender seemed like a smart guy who didn't want trouble.

Closing time was one o'clock and it was a quarter to when Jimmy settled his tab. I paid as I drank to be ready at a moment's notice. I let Jimmy get to the hallway before I joined a few other patrons making for the exit through the nearest set of doors. I stayed about fifteen feet behind him as he walked to his car. I halfway expected him to claim one of the cars that had tailed me, but instead he made straight for a Nash Roadster.

I closed the gap between us and as he opened his car door, I jabbed my gun hard into his right kidney, and snarled, "Don't turn around if you value having two kidneys."

"Hey, what is this?"

"One more outburst and I'll let you have it," I barked. "Now put your hands on top of the car." He did as I ordered and I said, "You were in the club Saturday and a guy with funny ears was talking to you. All I want to know is what you talked about."

"You're all wet, palsy. You got the wrong gee—"

I had expected his denial. Before he finished his last sentence, I was swinging my gun at his head. I clipped him on his ear and then shoved the barrel into his side as hard as I could. His body flattened against his car as he cried out in pain.

"You want to play, it's okay with me," I rasped.

He reached his hand up to his ear and stared at the blood seeping between his fingers. "You bastard," he exclaimed.

I put enough force behind my next shot to the side of his skull to drop him to his knees. "Had enough?"

He shook his head and put his hands over his head. I looked around the parking lot, but no one showed any interest in our little tête-à-tête.

"Talk before I spill your brains out on the bricks," I growled and pressed my gun to the back of his head.

"Hamm, he was asking about Hamm."

His declaration caused me to momentarily forget my next question. Red used the interlude to grab his door handle and steady himself. "Don't move if you know what's good for you," I ordered. "What did you tell him?"

"I told him who Hamm's boys were."

"I thought Hamm retired," I countered.

"That's what he wants everybody to think," he gasped in a defeated voice.

"And that's what you told him?"

He nodded 'yes.' "Did you tell Hamm about it?"

He started to say, "No," but changed his mind as I pressed harder with my gun. "Yeah, I told him."

"If I find out that you've told Hamm about our little chat, I'm going to finish the job I started," I said and conked him on the noggin. He crumpled in a neat heap next to his wagon and I strolled away.

I climbed in my loaner and muttered, "Verriet, you're an idiot," under my breath. Butters wasn't saying 'him,' he was saying, 'Hamm.' Now I knew where at least one of the old bosses stood. Whether Hamm knew about Boots' scheme didn't matter. He was getting ready to make a move. My guess was he had everything figured from the beginning and was waiting for Boots to clear a pathway for him to take over. *Whoever said these mobsters were stupid?* I was the stupid one.

Yeah, it fit. What was it I had thought about Hamm? Oh yeah, that he was 'a nice old man!'

Chapter Thirty-one

Tuesday

It was after two when I walked into my office. I decided to spend the rest of the night there with a chance Teri would call. The phone rang as I was retrieving an old fold-up cot from the back of the closet and a blanket. After I picked up the hand-piece, I heard a click and the line went dead. *Was it Teri?* Maybe she was too scared to talk now that she had reached me. If so, I was sure she'd call back, but after twenty minutes, I gave up hope.

I hadn't laid down for more than ten minutes before I heard the office doorknob rattle. I rolled off the cot, and flicked on the light switch.

"Is that you, Verriet?" a man's voice asked.

"Yeah, who is it and what do you want?"

"It's Tom, Boots wants to see you."

"Okay, tell him I'll come by in the morning," I replied before I realized it *was* the morning.

"He wants to see you now," he insisted.

"Look, I've had a long day and night. I'll swing by first thing."

He rattled the doorknob again, and pounded on the door so hard I thought the glass would break. "You're coming with me now if I have to break down this door," he shouted.

I considered giving him a glimpse of my gun and decided against it. Flipping back the door lock, I said, "C'mon in. You can wait long enough for me to get dressed can't you?"

Tom opened the door and grinned. "You got a dame in here or something?"

"I was sleeping, you bozo," I said and donned my shirt and pants. I slipped my gun under my belt while Tom sat in my desk chair and leafed through yesterday's paper.

Traffic was nonexistent at this hour. In ten minutes, he wheeled the big shiny black Cadillac to the rear entrance of Roscoe's and walked behind me up the stairs. He prodded me through the metal door with a gun he wielded in his meaty fist. I should have jumped him back at the office when I had a chance, but I irrationally figured I could manage whatever Boots had to throw at me. Tom rapped three times when we stopped outside Boots' office. Without waiting for a reply, he opened the door and motioned me inside.

Boots looked up from his papers. "Put him in the wood chair and tie him to it," with more than a little anger burning behind his eyes.

"Hey, what the hell is this?"

"Shut up wise guy, or I'll have Tom feed your teeth to you for breakfast," Boots barked. His entire manner had changed. Gone was the veneer of professionalism he had tried so hard to exhibit during our previous meetings. The brutal thug lying underneath the surface was revealed with all the ugly trimmings. Something had happened since my last visit and I had a good idea what it was.

Sam relieved me of my gun, tied my hands behind me, and my ankles to the chair legs. Secured, Boots stood up and walked around his desk until he faced me. He bared his teeth in an evil grin, and hissed, "One chance, wise guy, where is it?"

"I don't know. I haven't found it, yet," I answered truthfully.

Leaning back against his desk, Boots bit the end from a cigar, and spit it into a wastebasket. He struck a match and held the flame to the end of his cigar while he rolled it between his thick fingers. When he had the cigar glowing nice and red, he blew out the match and smiled at me knowing he had my full attention. Through a smoky haze he pointed the cigar at me. "I know 'bout you, Verriet. I asked around. Word is you're a smart dick who likes to play games. I think maybe you're playin' a game now. What say, boys, we find out if peeps is playin' games?"

"Shoot him in the knee, Boots! That'll make him spill," enthused Tom. "Ain't nobody not gonna talk with a shot up knee. Remember Pugsy? He'd still be talkin' if he could," he chuckled.

"Shut the loose mouth!" Boots shouted at him. He looked down at me, nodded his head, and said, "He does have a good idea, though. Nothin's more painful than a shot-up knee. Come here, Tom," he ordered.

Tom lumbered towards me with a smile, revealing his large yellowed teeth. Black matted hair covered the back of his hand that pointed the black bore of his.38 at my left eye.

Sweat broke out on my forehead and a rivulet ran down the middle of my back. "I told you I don't know where the case is," I blustered. Then I shouted, "Hold it!" as Tom moved his gun against my left kneecap. My stomach and leg muscles involuntarily tightened. A spasm of fear shot through my body as I shuddered.

"Hold it, damn it!" I shouted louder. "How can I know where the case is? Whoever has it killed Joe and nobody, not even the cops, knows who that is. When I find it, I'll tell you. It's what you hired me for, isn't it?"

"And what are you looking for, peeper?" Boots asked with a twisted grin.

"Money, books, or dope," I replied.

A sudden look of surprise appeared on his face and quickly vanished as his dull eyes took on a malicious gleam. "How do you figure?" he snarled.

"A little police birdie told me after Chuck was murdered."

The mention of the police snapped him out of his evil reverie, but not for long. He gave me a look of condescension and said, "Who killed Al Hewitt's boys?"

It was my turn to be surprised. "I thought you ordered the work."

He gave me another nasty grin and said, "Go ahead Tom, in the knee."

Sweat burst from more glands than I realized I possessed. The smell of fear reached my nostrils and my mouth became dry with a sick metallic taste.

Tom's fingers tightened on his gun's checkered grip. He leveled the barrel a foot from my left knee and squeezed the trigger. I screamed obscenities, only stopping when I realized nothing had happened. A wave of Tom's hot stale breath hit me as he convulsed with laughter. My face flushed red. My ears burned hotly and I swore like a stevedore.

Boots said, "Untie him boys. I figure him for bein' smart enough to talk before he'd take a dose of lead in the wheel."

Tom was still chortling as he untied my ropes. I gained my feet on the second try. My shirt clung damply to my body as I massaged my wrists and ankles.

Boots came around his desk, grabbed my cheeks between his fingers, and said, "You do like you said and find my goods, Verriet. Do as your told and I'll take good care of you. Who knows? When this trouble is over, maybe we'll be friends," he added with a light slap to my cheek.

"Yeah, Boots. I'll rush right home and add your name to my social register," I said with a sneer.

He backhanded me with a shot that sent me crashing against the wall. "Geez, some guys never learn," he said with a shake of his head.

I'd had enough. It was time to play one of my trump cards. "I lied, Boots. I know who killed Al's boys."

His head whipped around. "You really are nuts, you know that," he said in disbelief.

"I'm not kidding. I found out tonight, just before Tom picked me up. It was Hamm," I said assuredly.

He narrowed his eyes and asked, "Why didn't you say that a minute ago?"

"Because I didn't like how you asked."

"You lied with a gun to your knee?" he asked incredulously. "Now I know you're a crazy son-of-a-bitch."

"That was nothing compared to the fighting in the trenches."

"Yeah, I heard you was over there during the war. Heard you came back with a medal and a morphine habit, too," he scoffed before his face turned hard, like a bas-relief made of granite. "Tell me about Hamm."

I laid it out neat and quick for him. I finished by saying, "Call up St. Anthony's and see how Charles Butterworth is doing. Tell them you're his brother and you just found out he's there."

He opened a desk draw, pulled out a phone book and looked up the number. When he reached the hospital, he asked if they had a patient by the name of Butterworth. From the look on his face, they told him there was. A few more questions confirmed my story, at least that part of it, and he hung up.

"Describe the guy who told you about Hamm, again," he instructed.

"Tall, lanky guy, in his early to mid-thirties, well built, looks like he works out at a gym—a bit of bag work and maybe some sparring. He's got a lot of red hair."

"Sound familiar?" he asked Sam and Tom.

"Could be Jimmy Radditz. He used to run numbers for Hamm," Sam replied.

"I'll be damned," Boots shouted. "If Hamm is trying to double-cross me, I'll have his balls with spaghetti. Tom, find Radditz and make him spill. Sam, you watch Hamm's place. If Radditz confirms Verriet's story, join up with Sam and the two of you fetch Hamm to my boat. You know what to do from there," he finished with a satisfied look.

After Sam and Tom left, he muttered, "I give the guy a bundle and what's he do? The son-of-a-bitch turns around and tries to screw me. Ain't that a pisser?"

I nodded silent agreement. He seemed to forget I was still there as he continued his monologue. Finally, with a start, he looked up and said, "Don't you go gettin' any smart ideas, or I'll have Sam and Tom take you on a one-way cruise, too. Now, get outta here."

The back door only opened halfway when I pushed on it. I put my weight behind it and squeezed through. The dead weight holding the door was Tom, sprawled on the cement stoop. He was out cold, but his pulse was good when I bent over and felt under his chin. Sam lay at the bottom of the stairs in the same condition.

Quickly bending over, I examined them for wounds. None. Yet, someone had put their lights out only moments ago. I quickly glanced from side to side looking for their assailant. I didn't see anybody, but that didn't mean whoever was responsible wasn't lurking in the shadows. Hugging the side of Roscoe's, I crept to the end of the alleyway. At the corner, a car's lights suddenly popped on trapping me in their glare. Expecting the worst, I dove to the sidewalk and rolled back into the alley.

"It's okay, Verriet," I heard a voice say. "I'm Bob Wilks, Ray's partner. Get in and I'll give you a lift."

"Turn those damn lights off and show me your badge," I said. The car was a familiar two-tone Sunbeam.

Chapter Thirty-two

Wilks sat behind the wheel—a colored guy with premature gray highlighting his temples. He wore a black suit, white shirt and black bowtie. I remembered seeing him one other time wearing a derby in front of Dies' headquarters. *Man it takes some balls to be a police mole inside that group.*

"You knock those two out?" I asked as I climbed in the front seat.

"Yeah," he replied with a grin, "I wasn't so sure they wasn't goin' to do you harm when you comes out."

I opened the window and drew in the cool night air in deep breaths. An occasional star peaked out from behind scattered clouds as the full moon was setting. A funny feeling crept up my spine.

"How long were you waiting out back?" I asked, almost casually.

"I tailed you from your office. Been tailin' you for a while. But then you know that, you lost me on Sunday."

"Yeah, but I didn't know that was you. Did you go inside Boots' place after me?" I asked suspiciously.

"Yeah," he replied with a chuckle.

"What? You heard what was happening in there and you didn't lift a finger to save my ass?"

Wilks only smiled at my protestation. I called him a few nasty names embellished with an occasional curse and ending with a detailed description of his family tree.

"You were doin' all right on your own, man. Besides, I got to hear a lot more information that way," he replied with a big grin displaying large evenly spaced white teeth.

I cursed him again before I began to calm down. "Take me to my office."

"Yes, masser," he said in a Stepin' Fetchit voice.

"You're a real wet smack. I could have been killed back there."

"Yeah, then I could have nailed Boots fo sho," he said tritely. "But we's got his ass anyway, soon's he chills Hamm."

"That's some consolation. Remind me to thank the boys downtown."

He let out a horselaugh and slapped his knee. "I'll surely do that."

"That goes double for Ray. He told me you were working on a prostitution ring," I said still fuming. "So what are you going to do next about Boots and Hamm?"

"I'm not sure I oughtta be tellin' you that, but seein' as you been so much help, I guess it's all right. We ain't goin' to do nothin' but wait for them to kills each other. Then we's clean up whatever's left."

"The best money can buy," I said under my breath. "Does that include Dies?"

His face grew deadly serious. "Now that's somethin' you and me's gotta get straight. It won't be doin' no good you goin' around tellin' him 'bout me, now would it?"

"You mean like the way you let me sweat it out back there in Boots' office?"

"Tha's different. I'm under orders. Captain tol' me to gather information and watch you, nothin' more," he replied defensively. "Besides, Dies told everybody to keep an eye out for you. Said, you was one of the few decent white folk around and hows we needs every one of youse."

"Uh-huh. You sure kept an eye out for me back there. So what's Dies up to—I mean what's he planning to do about Boots taking over his numbers business?"

"He's smart. He's buyin' time to see what plays out. When the time's right, he'll make his move."

"And if he makes his move, what are you going to do about it?"

"Depends."

I was still digesting his information as I gave him directions to my office. The dark sky was giving way to a murky gray and it would be light in another hour or so. I invited him up for a drink, but he said he'd rather go home and catch forty winks.

After I climbed out of his car, I leaned over the door through the open window and asked him, "What would you have done if they had shot me back there?"

"I wouldda bust in and shot their eyes out," he replied gravely and sped off.

Chapter Thirty-three

Opening my bottom desk drawer, I retrieved a small toiletry case I keep for emergency occasions. In the bathroom across the hall from my office, I shaved, brushed my teeth, and washed up as best I could before I returned to my office and poured myself a cup of stale java.

After my second cup, I locked up and grabbed a quick bite at an all-night diner around the corner on Washington. I didn't realize how hungry I was until I finished off a plate of eggs with a steak and four pieces of dry toast.

Back in my office, I perused the latest edition of the *Tribune* I had picked up at Jaunty John's. The killing of Al's two stooges was relegated to page five. Nothing new was reported about the slaying.

Somewhere about the sports page, I must have dozed off because the next thing I knew my phone was ringing. I picked up the receiver and after I said 'hello,' Teri answered.

"Nick! Thank goodness, I finally reached you."

"Make it quick, Teri, someone may be listening in," I cautioned.

"Oh . . . I didn't think of that. Nick, you must know that I didn't have anything to do with that man's murder at the house."

"Never thought you did," I prevaricated.

"After I talked to you, I heard somebody try to get in again through the back door. I ran out the front and circled back to the garage to get my car."

"I don't know where you are Teri and I don't want to know. Stay out of the way until this clears up. Remember, the police are sure to check up on friends and relatives," I said in warning.

"I will, I promise. Nick?"

"Yeah?"

"When do you think this thing will be over?"

"I have a feeling it's coming to a head, probably in the next day or two. Then we can put the whole thing behind us and start over." I stressed earnestly.

161

"Sure, Nick," she replied weakly.

"You better get off the line now," I said and sighed contritely as I heard a click.

I wanted to tell her I loved her and wanted her, but it would have meant more trouble for us both if the cops were listening. An aimless longing, as if someone were ripping my heart from my chest, weighed on me. For a minute, I thought I was beginning to have a heart attack. My chest was tight and my whole body felt numb. I reached for the bottle of Old Granddad in my desk drawer, unscrewed the cap, lifted the bottle to my lips and took a long swallow. My throat burned in protest as the liquor went down. A few seconds later the pain in my chest eased, replaced by predominant exhaustion.

The cot was where I had left it, so I locked my office door, and snuggled in with gramps. The morning sun, shining brightly through my office window, blanketed me with warmth. After one more drink, I lay gramps to rest on the floor and fell asleep to the rhythmic street noise that marked the start of another business day.

When I awoke, I was drenched in sweat. The clock hands set the time at five in the afternoon. I badly needed a shower and change of clothes. I had missed the follow-up appointment with Doc Bax and needed to change my wound's dressing. I flagged down a hack to drive me to my apartment where I grabbed a cup of coffee and headed for the bathroom. Twenty minutes later, I emerged feeling refreshed and ravenous. It was a short walk to a neighborhood eatery where I ordered lake trout with a side salad.

With appetite sated, I began to leg it back to my apartment and discovered I had picked up a shadow—his reflection shown in the parked cars' windows lining the street. Without changing my gait, I entered my apartment building foyer, waited a few seconds, and quickly stuck my head out the door, looking left and right. A joe quickly turned around about thirty feet away and walked away from me down the street. His outline fit the gonzo who had tried to kill me in Wisconsin, the driver of the Dodge. He had too much of a head start for me to catch him.

Is he working for Boots? Or is this guy working for Hamm?
Neither made a whole lot of sense. Weighing the possibilities, I
decided the guy had to be connected directly or indirectly to
Boots.

I've never seen him at Roscoe's, *though that doesn't
necessarily mean anything. Boots may have told him to lie low. If
so, why did Boots pay me and then tell the guy to kill me? Maybe
the torpedo is acting on his own.*

Suddenly, a thought flashed into my consciousness. "Sure," I
exclaimed in wonder. "It fits. I'll be damned. That's got to be it,"
I said under my breath. "But it still doesn't make sense. It doesn't
connect up with Joe's murder, at least not how I have things
figured. If I take the guy who tried to kill me out of the equation,
who does that leave? The killer is after Boots' stuff and he or she
killed Chuck for the same reason."

In my apartment, I sat back and continued my latest line of
reasoning. Things became clearer as I stripped away various
players. When I took Chuck out of the equation, I narrowed the
possibilities down to a manageable number. The one puzzle piece
I wrestled with now was why anyone was earnestly trying to kill
me before I recovered Boots' money or drugs. The key lay with
the driver of the Dodge. I felt sure that tracing him would lead me
to Joe's killer. *Should I trap him, or have the cops pick him up?*

When I finished my mental perambulations, I reminded myself
I still had a personal score to settle with Joe's killer and Boots,
too. Nobody treated me to a party like the one in Boots' office
and got away with it. I freshened up a little, had a drink and
picked up the phone.

"I'm omniscient, you know that?" Ray announced when he
came on the line.

"Okay, Mr. Omniscient, tell me why I called," I said.

"You want to know what happened between Boots' boys and
Pete Hamm," he answered cockily.

"Bingo, give the man a cigar," I rejoined.

"Nothin' happened. The slab of Hamm ain't," he said with a
chuckle.

"Are you telling me the Hamm took it on the lam?"

"Oooh, I had that coming," he moaned. "Yeah, somebody must have tipped him off. We've been watching his place and it's as dead as a tomb."

"Makes sense," I acknowledged silently thinking about my encounter with Hamm's boy, Red Radditz. "So what does the soothsayer see in his crystal ball?"

"I see a half-witted private dick telling me what he's found out."

"Nothing Bob can't fill you in on. Did he tell you about last night?"

"Naw, the boss has got us workin' in shifts till we wrap this thing up."

I actually felt a little sorry for him. Shift work was for the birds, not to mention dealing with low-lifes day in and day out without let up. I decided to give him a break.

"This thing's coming to a head, I can feel it in my bones."

"Don't you mean bone? You probably need to get laid," he quipped back.

"You and Bob should go on the road, you know that? Bill yourself as the Two Blind Vice."

"A dick with a wit, or a half-one. What makes you think we're any closer to a bust?"

"Clues are adding up, or don't you know about those?"

"Keep it up and I'll have you thrown in the drunk tank."

"Listen, Ray, I'm serious. I've done some thinking and I'm close to some answers. Are you working the day shift the rest of the week?"

"Yeah, and don't go playing hero. If you're sure you got somethin', call me in on it, hear?"

I told him I would and he gave me his home phone number before he hung up. I decided he wasn't such a bad guy for somebody working vice.

Chapter Thirty-four

If my hunch was right, I needed to talk to somebody who knew Chuck well. Bobby was one possibility, and so was Gale, but I doubted Bobby knew enough about him, and I wasn't too positive about Gale, either. Regardless, I headed over to Roscoe's since I had promised Bobby I'd play with him one more time.

I found a spot near the entrance of a garage on Canal Street across the river. Most of the day workers had already left. Even the usual guys looking for handouts on the bridge had cashed in for the day.

Bobby was glad to see me when I tapped him on the shoulder. "Funny, ain't it?" he declared. "You're the only one I can count on and you ain't even a regular member of the band."

"Don't tell me you're missing somebody else."

"Not yet, but the boys are late and so's Gale. Man, my ulcer's turning cartwheels. Being in charge is for the birds."

"Bobby, I've been thinking about what you said earlier, and I'd like to sit down with you when I'm finished with this case." My declaration picked him up to judge by the broad smile on his face. "Right now, though, I need information. I know this is a long shot, but do you know who Chuck's supplier was or can you describe him?"

"I'm not sure, but Chuck used to talk to a guy who came in regularly. And you know Chuck, he wasn't exactly the friendly type."

"Have you seen the guy around since Chuck died?"

"Once or twice."

"What's the guy look like?"

"Small guy, 'bout five-and-half feet tall. Blond hair he keeps slicked back. Wears wire-rim glasses and has a moustache. You want me to ask the other guys if they know him?"

Before I answered, I felt a hand on my shoulder and turned to see Gale standing next to me. "Long time, no see," she said.

"Been busy workin'".

She airily dismissed my remark, and turned to Bobby. "What's the playlist for tonight, Bobby?" She examined the piece of paper he handed her, nodded her head, and said, "Good, I like the order. Nick, can I see you for a minute while I change?"

When we were safely entrenched in her small dressing room, she asked, "Are you working tonight or will I see you?"

"I told Bobby I'd play tonight. After that I'm all yours," I said half-heartedly. For some reason, spending the night with Gale wasn't as inviting a prospect as it had been on previous occasions.

A new life with Teri was all I wanted now. Gale was a gal I could fall back on if things didn't work out with Teri. She was a surrogate—maybe more, but my heart belonged to Teri. Using Gale wasn't fair to her, but she was using me, too.

She must have sensed something was up. "You don't seem overly enthusiastic about it."

"It's this case. Things are heating up."

"Do you mean you're on to something?" she asked anxiously.

"Yeah, I've got part of it figured out."

"What is it?"

"It has to do with the numbers racket."

My answer took the wind out of her sails. She wanted to hear results—me finding Boots' money. "I'll see you after the show," she said in a dismissive voice.

Bobby came over after I sat down and began to warm up. "The guys finally showed. You ready for tonight?" he asked and handed me the playlist.

Scanning the list, I nodded and said, "The usual, huh? You ever want to play something new?"

"Every night, brother, but the new stuff don't buy groceries or pay the rent."

"I don't know about that, Bobby. You hear some of the new stuff guys like Hoagy Carmichael are putting out? Seems like those guys may have hit on something."

"Yeah, but most of those guys already got a name," he countered.

"Some do," I conceded, "but if we want to keep playing jazz, we better think about a new style if we're going to make a career of it."

"Yeah, I suppose you're right," he agreed deferentially.

"It's that or go over to Europe," I stated.

He picked up at my mention of Europe. "Funny you should say that, Nick. I been thinkin' about Paris. Jimmy P. went over there last year and he wrote me saying it was the berries. And they ain't as prejudiced over there," he added speculatively.

"We'll see where the pieces fall out when this thing is over," I said as Gale made her appearance, wearing another new dress. *Man, this gal sure knows how to spend the do-re-mi.*

The fabric was made of a material that gave the appearance of molten metal. The back swooped down to her tailbone, the front revealing bountiful cleavage that was sure to elicit a Pavlovian response from the front row boys. Her sleek curves electrified all my nooks and crannies, and I fought hard not to swallow my epiglottis.

We went through a warm-up number before she retired to her dressing room while the band played the first set. I thought about Gale, Bobby, and Teri while I strummed chords four to the bar. When we finished, Bobby came over and asked quietly, "What's the matter, Nick? You ain't here tonight, man."

"I'm sorry, Bobby. I've got a lot on my mind. I'll do better the next set."

He gave me a troubled look that said, 'you better' before he laid down his horn and walked to the back of the stage. I grabbed a drink and took it back to my station, sat down and played around with a number I had been working on for quite a while. Before I knew it, the boys were ready for the next set. This time, I concentrated on the music and got a thumbs-up from Bobby when he signaled for us to take it up half a step during *King Porter Stomp*.

Gale came out and garnered good applause when she finished her first number. Most of the people clapping were guys who appreciated her curvaceous charms. After we polished off the set,

Bobby said, "Blondie's here," sotto voce as he passed by the piano on his way to the men's room.

I scanned the tables, but the bright stage lights made seeing the patrons nearly impossible. I casually went over to the bar, ordered a drink, and methodically scanned the room. Blondie sat at a table off to the side with three other guys, all sporting the latest ivy league glamor boy look. One of the guys looked nervously about the room before he reached in his pocket. He passed whatever he retrieved to the fellow next to him who immediately made an exchange under the table with Blondie.

The three guys hastily finished their drinks and beat leather with satisfied looks on their faces. During the break, I witnessed two more buys before it was time for the third set.

"Bobby, I'm going to sit out the first couple of numbers. I'll join you when Gale comes back."

He gave me a knowing look and said, "Be careful, even a trapped rat fight's for its life."

I acknowledged his advice with a nod and walked back to the bar. Blondie had picked the one spot in the joint where it was impossible to blind-side him. Somehow, I had to get him outside.

Mary, a pert gal with a great sense of humor, was serving up the drinks. We had talked music a couple of times when business was slow and I discovered she possessed an encyclopedic knowledge of modern music. I watched as she walked over to the server station carrying her tray in one up-tilted hand and deftly unloaded empty glasses onto the bar with the other. After she relayed her order to the bartender, I moseyed over to her.

"How's it goin' sweet cheeks?"

"Good, Nick. Hey what was that number you were playing earlier? I don't think I've ever heard it."

"Something I've been playing around with for a while."

"It's good, you should finish it."

"Thanks for the encouragement. Can I ask you to do me a favor?"

She gave me a wary look. "You can always ask," leaving the obvious part unspoken.

"There's a guy sitting at the far side of the room. He has blond hair and a mustache. You know him?"

"Yeah," she said skeptically, "name's Billy. He comes in regular. What do you want with him?"

"Business," I answered.

"Aw, Nick, don't tell me you're usin'," she said with a deflated look.

"Don't worry. I just want to ask him a few questions. It's a bit crowded in here. Would you tell him Boots wants to see him in his office?"

"Are you crazy? Boots'll fire me if he finds out," she said before she gave me a gamine smile and amended, "but I'll tell him a doll wants to see him out back. Will that do?"

"Like fine wine," I said and put a fiver on her tray.

"Give me a minute to make my rounds, okay?"

"Thanks, Mary."

A balmy night, the smoke from the band member's reefers still hung in the air by the back door. I smashed the naked bulb above the door with my gun butt, stood off to the side and waited. In a couple minutes, the door opened and a blond head poked out. Not seeing anyone, he stepped out further. I poked my gun into his short ribs, grabbed his arm and yanked him all the way outside.

Shutting the door behind me, I said, "Don't turn around. You can make this easy or hard, your choice."

"Man, take the money, it's yours," he said in a high tenor.

"I don't want your stinking money or your dope. Did Boots talk to you about your supplier?"

"I don't know who you're talking about," he cried.

"A tough guy, huh?" I hit him in the ear with the butt of my gun. He fell to his knees, grabbed his ear, and cried in disbelief, "You busted my eardrum."

I learned long ago a shot to the ear softens up even the toughest hood—attacking one of the senses always did the trick.

"I'm going to ask you one more time and if you don't come across, I'll do your other ear, and keep doing it until you have to learn sign language."

"Okay, enough, enough," he pleaded. "Yeah, a guy named Chuck set me up with Boots and I turned him on to my supplier."

Ka-chunk! One of the big puzzle pieces fell into place, confirming my suspicions. "There now. That wasn't so hard was it?" I grated. I ordered him to put his hands high on the back door and spread his feet. "Count to one hundred. If you turn around before you're done, I'll give you a third eye."

I jumped over the railing to the pavement and ran down the dark alley. When I reached the corner, I waited and watched. Blondie took a few minutes to compose himself. Light spilled out into the alley when he opened the back door and returned inside. I waited a couple more minutes before I hauled hips back to the bar. As I rejoined the band, I thought, *I'm close, real close to having the whole thing.*

Chapter Thirty-five

I resumed my seat at the bandstand and joined in playing the final bars of *In a Mix*, the number before Gale made her appearance. She walked to the center of the stage, her hips swaying invitingly. After the catcalls subsided, she began to lilt, *Some of These Days*.

The rest of the evening seemed to pass in a flash. I had the tiger by the tail, and now I had to figure out how to get him caged. The idea preoccupied my mental gyrations until Gale planted her chassis next to me.

"Nick, let's do one more number and scram."

I played *I Want to be Loved by You*, the easiest tune I could think of while I attempted to put the final puzzle pieces in place. Gale gave me a funny look, as if she questioned some hidden meaning behind my choice of song. She squeezed my knee when we finished, and said, "Let's go to your place tonight. I'm tired of staring at my four walls."

"All right, I'll pick you up out front," I said before she left to change. When I pulled up to the curb in front, I beeped the horn, and leaned over to open the door. She squatted and looked through the passenger window to see if it was me before she climbed in.

"Where's your car?"

"Had a little trouble with it, so I'm having a mechanic look it over."

We rode in silence to my apartment. Inside, she said, "Nick, pour me a tall drink. I feel like tying one on."

"Any special reason?"

"I've got a feeling."

"Woman's intuition, huh?" I said as I poured her a rye on the rocks.

"Yeah," she replied absently, walked over to my drafting table and picked up one of the scores. "What was that tune you were playing during break tonight?"

"Just a piece I've been working on for a long time. I call it *Siren's Song*," I said even though in my mind it was *Teri's Song*. "You like it?"

"Yeah, it was catchy. You should finish it."

I let out a laugh.

"What's so funny?"

"You're the second person tonight who told me that."

"Is arranging hard, Nick? It must be, since I don't know anyone else who does it."

"A lot of discipline is required and you never stop learning." I replied with a shrug. "After a while, things become easier. It takes a special gift. At first, you want to throw everything into the arrangements including the kitchen sink. Then you learn to be selective. There's a fine line between over-scoring and under-scoring. Listen closely to the really hot scores and you hear the genius."

"Are these scores for the band?" she asked holding up a couple music sheets.

"No, it's a personal project I've been working on for a while."

Gale laid the music down, walked over to my bookcase and perused the titles while she sipped her drink.

I picked up the music and scrutinized where I had left off scoring parts for two B-flat clarinets. That's when the answer hit me in a blinding flash. I stopped breathing while my mind raced with the idea, seeing if all the miscellaneous pieces tumbled into place.

"Damn, it can't be. It just can't be. Can it?" I asked absentmindedly.

Gale gave me a funny look. "What's the matter, Nick?"

My nerves went into overdrive. Putting my hand to my forehead, I stood still and considered the implications of my discovery. Oblivious to Gale, I thought back to the beginning of the case and began to refit all the little details together. Damn. Every little piece fit, and I knew I had it. "I'll be damned," I said absently, and mentally reviewed everything again.

There was a tug at my sleeve. "Nick, you look like you've seen a ghost," she said vociferously. "What's the matter?"

"I know it all. I know every damned thing," I exclaimed numbly.

She looked scared when I turned my focus on her. She finished her drink in a single gulp. "You mean you know where Boots' money is?"

"Uh-huh."

"That's g-great," she stammered hesitantly before she sashayed over to my cellaret, poured two fingers of rye in her glass and threw the drink down without taking a breath. After she regained control of herself, she put her hand on my arm. "Now we can get it and dump this town."

"This calls for a celebration," I agreed, grabbing the bottle and refilling our glasses.

"Where is it and when do we get it?"

A faint smile graced my lips. "It's buried on Joe's property. And *we* aren't going to get it, *I* am. It could be dangerous and I don't want you getting involved."

She looked at me as if she was appraising a pound of ground sirloin at the butchers. She wasn't sure if I was feeding her a line or playing straight. I could read the struggle behind her eyes. *Should she trust me or not.*

"So when are you going to dig it up?"

"Tomorrow," I answered quietly.

"So we can leave tomorrow?" she urged.

"Right after I retrieve it," I confided to pacify her. All my hopes were with Teri and how she'd receive the truth.

"I better go home and start packing then," she proclaimed ecstatically.

"There's no hurry. The money's not going anywhere."

"Yeah, but I'll have to let my landlord know. And then I have to contact the utility companies to stop my service, and—"

Cutting her off, I said, "Yeah, I guess you're right. I'll drive you home."

"No, I'll call for a cab. You've had too much to drink. Why don't I come over tomorrow when I'm all through packing?"

"That'll be swell," I replied mechanically.

She pulled my head down to hers and gave me a long kiss to seal our pact. With a big smile she said, "Just think, Nick, by this time tomorrow everything will be so different, so inviting. We'll be on our way to Europe," and gave me another kiss. "I'm so excited, I don't think I'll be able to sleep."

After Gale left, I sat in the living room in the dark and mentally retraced the case from the beginning again. It took on a surrealistic imagery, as if I were viewing a slideshow in reverse. Pictures raced across my vision, frame after frame, everything I had witnessed from Gale's kiss to her visit in my office with Boots' boys. Gale was right about one thing—by this time tomorrow, everything would be different, but not according to anyone's plans.

Chapter Thirty-six

Wednesday

I slept like the dead. Having solved the puzzle, my brain was no longer working overtime to make sense of all the pieces. I didn't wake up until three. After a quick shave and shower, I went out for a bite to eat and returned to my apartment. I cleaned my gun, filled my pockets with extra cartridges, and tucked my gat under my waistband.

I called Gale first and told her I'd stop by after I had the money. She didn't protest and that spoke volumes.

Powers was next on my list. He was in his office when I called. He agreed to meet there an hour later. As an after-thought, I went to my hall closet and dragged out an old pump action 12-guage my old man had used to hunt pheasants. After a good cleaning and oiling, I stuck it back in its case with a hand full of shells. I did a last minute inventory, trying to think of anything else I might need. I had already stuffed a flashlight and a couple of flares into a sack along with a thermos of coffee. Satisfied everything was in order, including a note to my landlord in the event I didn't return, I went to the garage.

Ray Stepson was standing in Powers' office when I walked in. Powers' picked up the stacks of files adorning his desktop and set them on the floor as Ray and I took a seat in the wood chairs facing his desk.

Without exchanging preliminaries, I gave them both a rough sketch of what I had figured. Finished, I asked Powers, "Do you have any pull with the cops in the Lake Geneva area?"

"I know Captain Kelly. We go fishing together every summer. Why?"

"Because that's where the proof lies."

"You want to be a little more specific about that, Verriet?" Powers asked.

"Everybody's been looking for what Boots lost. It's up there, along with Joe's killer."

"You sure about this, because if you're wrong or thinking of pulling a fast one, I'm going to have Kelly run you in until I can send somebody up there to fetch you back."

"Positive."

Powers turned to Ray and asked, "I think you should handle this. I'd like to, but my manpower is stretched thin with these mob killings. You okay with that?"

"Sure, Lieutenant. Me and Verriet's great pals," Ray said with a sarcastic grin.

Powers grunted, picked up his phone, and placed a call to Kelly.

After he provided Kelly with some background, he got down to particulars with him. A few minutes later, he asked me, "Got anything else for us?"

"Get the directions to his office for me."

Powers didn't like taking orders from anybody, but he wrote down the directions on a pad of paper, ripped off the sheet and tossed it to me. After he hung up, he reluctantly said, "If this turns out, I suppose I'll owe you one."

"Thanks, I hope I won't ever need the favor."

"You will," he snapped.

Chapter Thirty-seven

The sun was making a curtain call behind scattered clouds as I drove north on Lake Shore Drive. A beautiful summer evening, I wished my old beater was available for the trip. Traffic was heavy until I reached the far North Side. Another thirty minutes, I crossed the state line where I turned off the main highway.

When I realized I had picked up a tail, I grinned. I'd have been alarmed if my shadow wasn't there. His appearance only went to confirm what I already knew. My tag-along stayed about five hundred yards back, and slowed when I signaled for the turn. I hit the accelerator and watched as he, too, turned and then faded back. I slowed down and he reappeared on a straight section of highway. I drove leisurely. It wasn't time to lose him, yet.

Another twenty miles brought me to the little town of Lake Geneva. As I hit the outskirts of the small hamlet, I flicked off my lights and stomped on the ethyl until I came to a road on my right. An old two-story brick building with a Red Oaks Lumber Company sign out front graced the near corner. I turned a sharp right, parked and waited. My tail slowly rolled by my position. Leaving my lights off, I turned at the next corner to be on a parallel street. I raced to gain a lead so that when I turned back onto Main Street I would be facing him. I parked in the first open space between two cars on Main and waited.

The Dodge crossed over Main Street, and skirted out of sight. I swore and readied for the unlikely event he'd come up behind me. Luck was with me as a couple of minutes later he rounded the corner back onto main Street, slowed and pulled up to the curb at the far end of the block from my position. He climbed out and swiftly walked to a wood telephone booth in the middle of the block. I eased open my car door, crouched down, and circled my car. My hat pulled down and suit coat collar flipped up, I approached him.

I was thirty feet from the telephone booth when a sudden screeching of tires penetrated the night air. From the same direction my pursuer had come, a car hurtled around the corner.

The car's headlights outlined my silhouette on the building to my right. I lamped a glimmer of metal sticking out a back window seconds before I dove behind a parked car, scraping my hands on the bricks and banging my shoulder. I yanked out my heater. The sound of gunfire reverberated in two quick bursts before the car sped past my position. The car was a black Cadillac, Boots' boys' car.

Picking myself up, I tucked my gun back in the holster, and rubbed my raw, gritty palms on my handkerchief. The collapsed body of my pursuer lay in a pool of blood on the sidewalk in front of the phone booth. I walked swiftly toward him and saw he had taken both shotgun blasts in the chest, his shirt a solid red.

I knelt and vainly felt for a pulse. His wallet was in his rear pocket. Gingerly, I opened it and found a P.I. license in the name of Jason McAllister. A piece of paper fell out when I checked his wallet's side pockets. I snatched the paper off the sidewalk before replacing his wallet.

I examined his face, dotted red by the lead shot. Yeah, he was the gazabo who had tried to kill me—twice. The guy who tried to drive me off the road, and then shot at me the first time I was assaulted in the garage. Now I knew why he had looked familiar. Our paths had crossed a few years back. He had a reputation for playing fast and loose with the law. All private dicks bend the rules out of necessity from time to time, but he liked to play faster than most by setting both sides against his own middle. A profitable game if you could pull it off, but the stakes had always been too high for me to try it.

A man ran from across the street and joined me. "Man, I wish I hadn't seen that!" he said in a shaky voice. I looked up at the gawking citizen. He was ghost white and trembling like a leaf. Two other people walked hesitantly over to join us.

A siren wailed in the distance. In a minute, two cops arrived. One cop bent over McAllister, confirmed he was dead, and told his partner to call headquarters. He located McAllister's wallet, looked at the license for a minute and then opened the money compartment. He extracted a small cache of Clevelands. The cop let out a low whistle and I nodded to myself knowingly.

Without my saying a word, the witness let loose with a description of the shooting, rambling on and on until one of the cops shut him up with a string of pointed questions. The witness gave them all the details. He was a local shopkeeper who happened to be locking up at the time of the incident.

Being the first on the scene, the storeowner and I had to go to the station to give our statements. The cops were reluctant to let me go when they learned I was a P.I. from Chicago, too, but they had such an obsequious local witness they had little choice after I merely reiterated his story.

The police station was two blocks from Main Street, so I leisurely strolled back to the scene. The black Dodge sat where McAllister had parked it, the key still in the ignition. I opened the trunk and discovered a lot of wire and phone stuff. Finding the cache of equipment removed the last shred of doubt that McAllister was the guy who had tapped my office phone. There was no suitcase, but I hadn't expected to find one.

I tossed the key inside, walked back to my car, and sat thinking. McAllister was the wild card in the puzzle. I reached in my pocket and straightened out the crumbled piece of paper that had fallen out of his wallet. The final puzzle piece fell into place like tumblers in a safe, and I swore under my breath. For once, I wished I hadn't solved a case. Now that all the cards were on the table it was time to see who was going to walk away with the winnings. I wasn't greedy, I'd settle for just being able to walk away.

Chapter Thirty-eight

I drove with heavy reticence to Joe's cabin. The waxing moon cast a crazy chiaroscuro pattern through the thick stands of pine that bordered his property along the sandy lakeshore. Switching off the motor, I let the car coast down the dirt incline and pulled up next to the cabin. I sat, collected my thoughts and waited. Knowing I might not walk away from the inevitable showdown, my mind wandered, thinking back to the times Teri, Joe, and I had shared together as kids.

Those were good times, the best in my life. A yearning for my youth engulfed me in a forlorn blanket of pity. With one aching memory, came another, each with more longing than the last until I felt suffocated. Breathing deeply of the cool, clean, night air, I cleared my head and numbed myself for what I was about to encounter. The air was heavy with pine scent, and the incessant humming of bugs, sporadically interrupted by croaking bullfrogs, helped to calm my racing thoughts.

I climbed out of the car and walked around the cabin to the lakeside. The moon shone brightly off the still water. I stepped up to the porch, opened the screen door and retrieved the dirty white beekeeper's outfit. Short for my frame, I struggled into it, slouching down to secure the collar. Grabbing the mesh hood and gloves, I started for the hives.

I examined the first beehive for frame seams. Not finding any, I fiddled with the wood-slat sides, and when that failed, I tried lifting up on the bark-encrusted roof. The whole top was hinged on one side. I flipped the top all the way back and looked inside. The bees began to come to life, their buzzing steadily increasing, as I probed the inside with one of my gloved hands. I quickly closed the top and went to the next hut.

The same operation yielded the same result with more bees joining the war party. I continued through the next three pairs of huts. At the ninth hut, I noticed something different. Someone had removed the inside panels. I reached in and felt a rectangular object. My breathing increased as I struggled to get a firm grip with my gloved hand on the object. Pulling it out, alligator-hide gleamed in the moonlight.

With a sigh of relief, I set Boots' errant case down on the ground. My exultation was short-lived. As I flipped back the roof, the hut next to me suddenly exploded into a cloud of splinters, and a loud gunshot retort echoed off the trees. I reached for my gun and with a sick feeling realized I couldn't retrieve my gat until I gained a position of safety to undo the coveralls. I clumsily ran hunched over to the far end of the apiary houses, and glanced back around the last hive.

Two gunmen were silhouetted in the moonlight, too dark for me to make out their features, but to judge from their outlines, I knew they were Sam and Tom. Tom held a shotgun and Sam a revolver. Tom fired again when he was thirty feet away. I dove behind the next hut when the one I had just abandoned disintegrated into an angry swirl of bees.

The pair spread out and advanced steadily. In a few seconds, I'd be trapped, the white suit made a perfect target. I had to do something fast. When they were ten yards away, I made a desperate dash, weaving in and out of the row of huts nearer to the pines. Another shotgun blast hit the hive on my left and I felt shotgun pellets sting my left shoulder. My movement caused the already ripped material to further tear, opening to my waist. Stings from another source made me move yet farther away from the house—the efficient little buggers having found the split in my suit.

Sam and Tom were about ten feet from the first row of hives when they met the angry bees. I heard screams and another shotgun blast. Without hesitation, I ran to the trees where I slipped off a glove, unzipped the suit, and retrieved my gat. Gun in hand, I clumsily re-zipped the suit and risked a quick look.

Tom let out another terrible, strangled scream and stumbled towards the cabin. He slipped and fell to the ground with a loud moan. Sam was zigzagging around the huts, waving his hands frantically in a futile attempt to ward off the mad swarm. When he stepped out from the huts, I cut loose three quick shots. He spun around violently and dropped to the ground. I approached Sam's prone framework slowly until I lamped him. One of my shots had caught him in the throat, another in the chest.

I peered around the beehive. Tom was lying like a spent missile where I had last seen him fall. I slowly made my way forward, gun at the ready. He lay face down and didn't respond when I nudged him with my foot. I flipped him over and bees flew out of his open mouth. His face was a swollen crimson red, dotted and puffed beyond recognition by innumerable bee stings. He looked like somebody had pumped his face full of gas and used it for a pin cushion. His eyes were swollen shut and his tongue lolled out grotesquely. I waved my arms over him to ward off the bees that continued their deadly barrage.

I walked back and retrieved the suitcase. I stuck my gun in one of the bee suit's pockets, retrieved Tom's .38, and put it in the other pocket. I laid the suitcase on top of Tom, grabbed his feet, and began to drag him toward the cabin. Halfway there, I stopped to catch my breath. I brushed away the unrelenting bees again, took ahold of his feet once more, and pulled him up onto the porch.

I opened the door into the main room, stripped off the bee suit, and halted as a voice boomed, "That's far enough." Boots was concealed in the dark interior of the cabin. "Put your gun on the floor and kick it over here you son-of-a-bitch."

I took out Tom's gun and did as he asked. He struck a match and lit a lantern sitting on top of the kitchen table. He motioned with his gun for me to sit at the table, reached down and picked up Tom's gun. He took a couple of steps around me and glanced through the doorway to the porch. When he spotted Tom, I thought his eyes were going to pop out of their sockets.

"Jeez! What the hell did you do to Tom?"

"Nothing. The bees got him."

"Bees?"

"Yeah. Joe kept bees. Those are bee hives," I said nodding toward the lake. "Tom was probably highly allergic to their stings, but who knows, that many stings would probably kill anybody," I added, uncomfortably shifting in my chair. From the angry look on his face, I feared he was going to trigger the gun at any moment he pointed at my gizzard.

"What about Sam?"

"Dead."

Boots kept the gun on me as he shuffled backwards through the doorway. He turned and left my vision for a mere split second before he returned with the suitcase in his free hand, not giving me enough time to retrieve my own gun from the discarded bee suit.

A triumphant look on his face, he proclaimed, "Looks like this is the end of the line, Verriet. You should have delivered my case instead of playing games."

"I don't think so, Boots, because someone would have stopped me from giving it to you."

"You're right about that peeps," he said with a grin.

"The same person who's going to stop you from leaving with it," I said trying not to sound as scared as I felt.

With a little laugh he said, "Oh yeah. And who's that?"

"Him," I said nodding behind him.

"You gotta do better than that," Boots scoffed.

"No, he doesn't," Joe said and prodded Boots forward with a gun behind his left kidney. "Drop it, Boots," he ordered.

"So you two are in this together, huh? I shouldda known," he said with a shake of his big head.

"I said, drop it," Joe repeated tensely.

Boots had guts, I'll give him that. He pivoted, his rod tightly clutched in his meaty fist. Joe's mug blanched a sickly pallor; his gun wavered in his hand. He clamped his other hand around the gat to steady his aim. "Drop it now or I'll shoot you. I mean it, Boots. I'm not kidding," he screamed frantically.

Boots grinned and kept turning to face him. Joe screamed again before he delivered on his promise. The first bullet tore into Boots' midsection. The second went through his shoulder. The impact spun him so he faced me wearing a querulous look, as if he couldn't believe his number was up. He tried to turn back, his gun still raised.

Joe pumped three more doses of lead into his torso. Boots staggered backward and slid down the wall to the floor, his legs splayed out in front of him, a silly grin glued on his face. His eyes fluttered, and his head rolled to one side until his chin came to rest on his massive chest. His body jerked once and his hand opened, finally releasing its hold on his gun. A dull thud resounded as metal struck the wood floor.

Joe's body shook and he had to lean against the doorframe to keep from collapsing.

"Nice work," a woman's voice said from behind the screen door.

Chapter Thirty-nine

Gale stepped into the room holding a .22 in her right hand. I wasn't surprised by her presence. She was a smart gal who had learned the hard way to always hedge her bets. She worked all the angles. Her presence was a total surprise. I figured she was leading Boots on, pretending to be his pawn while really working on her own. I wasn't sure if I was happy she had arrived with Boots or not.

I turned to her and shouted, "Why did you wait? He could have shot me," in an outraged voice.

"Relax, sweetie, I had him covered."

"So that's how it is, huh?" Joe asked. His earlier frenzied look of anxiety replaced with a determined hardness. I had trouble seeing the man I once knew through his mercilessly wrathful countenance.

"Yeah, Joe. It's a damn shame, but you hold my meal ticket," she said matter-of-factly. "Give it up, Joe, and walk out of this alive."

He scrunched up his face and slowly shook his head. "I don't think you've got the guts," he said and moved the gun back and forth from Gale to me and back again.

I figured the longer I kept him talking, the more chance we had at getting out of this alive. "Yeah, Joe. I'll admit it took me a while, but I finally got it. Tell me why, old friend. What did I ever do to you?"

"Teri. You took Teri," he answered with a wrathful gleam in his eye.

"What are you talking about? She married you, not me," I retorted venomously.

"Yeah, but she was always yours. She even used to say your name at night," he said with a dark reminiscent scowl.

"But she must have loved you to marry you," I insisted.

"She only turned to me when you got shot up and came back hooked on morphine," he growled. "You were always the one.

You had the talent and Teri. All I ever had was a two-bit jazz band on its last leg. This is my second chance, don't you see?"

"I'm sorry for you, Joe, but this isn't your second chance," I averred and nodded toward Gale. Gale had been quiet the whole time, thinking over Joe's news about Teri and me.

Joe gave her a look and turned his attention to me. "Why isn't this my chance?"

"You can shoot one of us, but not both without one of us drilling you."

"You're bluffing. You don't have a gun."

"Oh no? Look at the gun I gave Boots—it was Tom's .38. You know I pack a .45," I said and nudged at my hand in my suit coat pocket at him."

He looked at my ersatz handgun and fatalistically shrugged with a mad gleam glistening in his eyes. "At least I'll have the satisfaction of killing you."

"Sure, go ahead, Joe. But answer me one question first."

"What?" he asked with narrowed eyes.

"Did you hire a P.I. named Jason McAllister?"

"Yeah, I hired him. So what?"

"Did you pay him to kill me?"

"No, that pleasure is going to be all mine."

"That's what I figured. You hired him to keep tabs on me, but he had other plans. I was slow on the uptake. I couldn't figure out who would hire a P.I. until last night when I finally accepted the seemingly impossible and knew you were still alive."

He digested the information and glanced wildly around the room. Gale, her face froze in a mask of fear, desperately cried, "Nick, look at him. He's crazy. Shoot him," she pleaded.

Damn, she's bought into my bluff about having my gun.

Joe looked at her like an entomologist might look at a new bug species. I nodded for her to go into one of the bedrooms. She gave me an uncertain look and took one-step before Joe blurted, "Hold it. One more move dolly and you'll be the first one I shoot."

186

Gale couldn't bring herself to pull the trigger. Her hands shook so violently I was afraid she was going to drop the pistol. Now that I had bluffed, I was committed to playing the hand out.

"You've been working all the angles right from the beginning, haven't you, old buddy?" I said without hesitating. "First, you played Chuck and made him think you were going to supply him. You're the one who sent him to your place to throw everybody off the trail and to pin things on Teri and me."

Joe's face hardened into an angry scowl. "You were always the smart guy," he said savagely.

I seized the moment, and continued, "By covering enough bases, you figured to wind up with the suitcase and make tracks while everybody else fought it out. It was a smart move involving Chuck and an easy way to eliminate him since he was getting harder for you to control."

Joe nodded a silent assent.

"Yeah, you hoped the cops would pick up Teri, too, and eliminate another player in the game. Once you killed Chuck with your .22, you had Teri where you wanted her—in the frying pan with me. You set us all up so we'd end up fighting each other while you walked away with the spoils.

"I'll let you in on a little secret. You hired McAllister to keep tabs on me, but you didn't count on him double-crossing you and taking things into his own hands. He was the joker in the deck. He knew something big was up since it involved Boots. Rumors on the street reached him and he figured out whatever was in the suitcase was worth going after. Like the rest of us, he must have guessed either drugs or money was involved. He tried to kill me twice to eliminate his competition, thereby increasing his own odds of finding the missing goods. When he wasn't successful, he kept a watchful eye on me night and day. He even tapped my office phone.

"He trailed me up here. Without a doubt, he intended to grab the goods and murder you and me and whoever else stood in his way, but luck was with you tonight, buddy—I told Boots I was being followed and he had his lads watching out for McAllister.

They finally caught up with him and iced him before he could come after you."

His attention was riveted to me, mulling over my information. I gave Gale another meaningful look. *Move dammit. He's not paying attention to you. Now's your chance!*

I had Joe listening to my every word, just where I wanted him, but Gale was still too scared to move. Now my only chance was to keep Joe occupied, to keep talking until I could get the drop on him.

"Yeah, McAllister was working strictly for himself. You hadn't counted on that, did you? You figured you had Boots, me, Chuck—even Gale, wrapped around your finger," I smirked.

Gale's shouted hysterically, "Shoot him. Shoot him now, Nick."

Dammit, Gale, when are you going to realize it's all a bluff?

"But you were ready for that eventuality weren't you?" I said and pulled the piece of paper out of my pocket. "Here," I said motioning to Joe. "This paper has the directions to this cabin. I found the paper in McAllister's wallet after Sam and Tom cooled him in town. It's in your handwriting, just like the note you left in Chuck's sax case and the one you left after you murdered that poor tramp.

"You left too many notes, Joe. Your notes helped me piece together the puzzle. That was another mistake. You gave McAllister directions to find the cabin when I came up here. It was your insurance in case I lost him. Little did you realize that he figured you hid Boots' case here, too. You underestimated him and it nearly cost you your life, but then you were going to kill him, too, weren't you?"

He responded with a small uncaring shrug.

"And I'll let you in on a big surprise, pally. Teri loves you, not me. She was broken up when she found out you had died. She wouldn't have blown town if I meant anything to her. You were all wet about her lack of feelings for you, and that was your biggest gaff. Put down the gat and we'll all walk away from this. You can have Boots' drugs. Gale and I won't even go to the cops.

We're packed and ready to go overseas. You'll never see us again."

I had bought time in the hope that Joe would see reason, but my hopes quickly vanished by the wild look he gave me. He was beyond reason. My remaining hope was for Gale to calm down and make an attempt to get out of harm's way. But instead of making any effort to extricate herself from the deadly dilemma, she seemed torn between summoning the courage to shoot Joe and the abject fear of dying.

"What are you waiting for, Nick?" Gale cried.

Her outburst snapped Joe back to the present. He let out a maniacal laugh, and his heater barked twice. Ka-chow! Ka-chow! Gale looked down in disbelief at the spreading red spots on her dress. A myriad of expressions ranging from denial to terror formed on her face in the brief moment before she collapsed.

With a broad arc of my arm, I swept the lantern off the tabletop in Joe's direction and scrambled for the porch. I dived over Gale, held her dead body close to me while Joe let loose with another round. He hit Gale's body with the first shot and his second hit me in my left thigh.

I rolled to the porch while he reloaded. Frantically, I reached for my gun still in the bee suit pocket lying in a heap on the floor. I got a hold of it, aimed and fired just as Joe appeared in the doorway. My first shot slammed him into the doorframe and my second and third shot hit him square in the chest. He looked at me, and with a tired smile said, "Funny ain't it, Nick. Who would have thought we'd end up like this, huh?"

I grabbed him as he toppled over and eased him to the floor. I cradled his head in my arms while his eyes turned glassy. Blood poured from his mouth and his breathing came in labored bursts. Red bubbles formed on his lips. "S-s-sorry. Tell Teri I'm s-sorry," he gasped and died in my arms.

I closed his eyes and sat holding him for who knows how long. It might have been ten minutes or two hours. Eventually, a throbbing in my leg brought me back to the present. I looked at my pants leg plastered to my wound. I ripped my pant leg open for a closer inspection. No arterial damage, I'd live. This was the second war I'd survived.

Easing Joe's body to the floor, I crawled over to the leather case and opened it. Six circular tins were inside. I pried one open. The tin was packed with white powder. Opening the bag, I wet the tip of my little finger and stuck it into the powder. The white crystals that adhered to my finger were bitter to the taste. The bees had harbored a bitter honey, as close to pure heroin as I had ever witnessed.

I placed the lid back on the tin and limped outside. When I reached the trees at the edge of Joe's property, I searched the grounds. I found what I was looking for, a medium sized boulder. Pulling it loose with my hands, I placed the tin underneath in a cavity I scratched out of the dirt with a stubby tree branch.

I made a mental picture of the spot and counted the trees, marking the approximate entrance point into the woods. Hobbling back to the cabin, I washed my hands and brushed off my cloths before I lit one of the flares I had packed in my car. In minutes, Kelly and Ray showed. While we waited for an ambulance to take me to the hospital, I turned over the case of dope and gave them a quick rundown.

The doctor on emergency call tended to my wound and administered a sedative that knocked me out until two the next day. Then a seemingly endless line of law enforcement officials paraded in and out of my room until the head nurse finally shooed the last of them away when my supper arrived. They released me the next day to answer additional questions by the local gendarmes at the Lake Geneva police station, the county sheriff, and the state police. Kelly took pity on me and took me home when his shift ended. His wife cooked dinner for us before making up a bed for me in a spare bedroom.

I was finally free to return to Chicago the following morning with the understanding I was to report to Powers as soon as I hit town. Another day of questioning by the homicide boys ensued with more of the same by Ray and the vice squad. Looking back on the whole thing, I suppose I was fortunate to crawl out from under the entire affair with nothing more than a sore leg and memories which would haunt me for the rest of my life.

Chapter Forty

Monday

Teri had called me Sunday after she read the papers. I agreed to meet her for lunch the next day in Uptown where she had been staying with a friend. We picked out a booth in the back of an eatery where we could talk quietly without worrying about eavesdroppers. I gave her a rough sketch of everything that had happened at the lake.

When she asked me how Joe became involved in the affair, I said, "Somewhere along the line, Joe must have caught on to what Boots was up to. Boots was taking over the numbers racket in Chicago. Everybody figured Boots was consolidating the old mob bosses' numbers operations into one efficient operation, but he had bigger plans. He was going to use the numbers set-up for drug distribution. Nobody, including me, could figure out why he didn't follow the usual mob plan of eliminating the competition. He absorbed the competition, even paid them more and promised them better days if they stuck with him. It was all about the drugs.

"One of the mob bosses Boots thought he had bought off, a sweet old man named Hamm, tried an end-around on him and that had me confused for a while, but once I figured out the distribution angle, everything fell into place. That's when I knew Boots had lost either the money he was going to use to purchase the drugs or the drugs he had already purchased.

"Joe got wind of what Boots was up to. He probably figured Boots used Chuck's and Honey's connections to work his way up the distribution chain of command. How Joe interceded and grabbed the heroin shipment, we'll never know. But Joe was smart enough to realize he crossed the point of no return once he snatched the heroin. I'm not sure exactly what Joe planned up front besides stealing the drugs, and maybe he didn't even plan that. Maybe the opportunity arose on the spur of the moment and he just reacted.

"I don't think he wanted to kill anyone when he first stole the case. But don't get the wrong idea. Joe definitely became unhinged somewhere along the line. You said he hadn't been acting himself for some time so he must have been mulling over things for quite a while. But I suspect the idea to use the bum as a decoy occurred to him later—when he ran into the two bums scavenging through the trash in the alley behind the house where he was hiding out. My guess is Joe got to know the two hoboes a little and that's when he figured a way out from under—a way to escape Boots' clutches using me as a scapegoat."

"But you never did a thing to him, Nick. You were his best friend," Teri exclaimed.

"That's not how he saw it. First, I think the guilt of marrying you gnawed away at him from the beginning. Eventually he twisted the whole thing around until he came to see himself as the victim." I didn't mention to her what Joe had revealed to me at the cabin—how she never stopped loving me. It wouldn't change anything now. It would only make things harder on her.

"So Joe killed one of the bums?" she asked incredulously.

"Uh-huh. First, he called me up and set the stage. He kept the bum drunk for some time until he reached me. Then, he timed things, killing the poor guy just before I arrived. When I got there, we talked for a while. He made it look like he had been drinking a lot so I wouldn't question the doctor's results which revealed the bum's high blood alcohol content.

"He also feigned wanting my help. During our talk, he used the pretext of running out of cigarettes to go to the kitchen to fetch more. Instead, he waited in the kitchen long enough until he knew I'd get suspicious and come looking for him when he didn't return. He knocked me out and worked over my knuckles to make it look as though I had killed the bum.

"I didn't find an empty pack of cigarettes on his victim's body, nor did I find any cigarettes in the kitchen when I searched the house later. It should have been enough to tip me off to the truth, but I was slow on the uptake. I never considered Joe capable of

193

killing anyone. That was my big mistake. Everyone has a breaking point.

He beat the bum beyond recognition and once he switched clothes and personal belongings with him, who was to say it wasn't Joe? Remember how the body in the morgue didn't have a recognizable face? You identified the body by the clothes and ring, didn't you?"

She nodded in silent agreement, having a hard time digesting it all.

"And Joe killed the band player in our house, too?" she asked in a small voice.

"Yeah, you either heard Joe or Chuck trying to get in that night when you called and told me about hearing an intruder. Chuck was acting according to Joe's directions. I suspect Joe was stringing Chuck along, possibly with dope. He baited Chuck to go to your house. Joe thought killing Chuck in your home would implicate you in his murder. By then, Joe was completely over the edge. He shot Chuck with the .22 you thought he owned."

"Yes, but why did Gale come to you in the first place?"

"Good question. I don't think everything went according to Joe's plans," I answered. "At first, I think Joe was hoping to steal the heroin, sell it and leave town, but Gale entered the picture. Somewhere along the line, she got wise to what Joe was up to. She figured Joe either took Boots' money or drugs. Remember, she was close to Chuck. They had a history that began in Detroit. Gale's ultimate plan was to find the money and get lost—to start a new life for herself. Gale was a smart gal. She had plans of her own. Unfortunately, even the best-laid plans go awry.

"Joe wanted his revenge on me, but when the cops didn't immediately put the bracelets on me for his mocked-up murder, his plan began to unravel. Joe was new at the game. He didn't have a contingency plan. Things didn't work out as he hoped, and he found himself stuck in Chicago with nobody to pass the blame onto unless the cops hooked me. As more time passed without me being jugged, Joe must have decided to turn up the heat and Chuck was the next best candidate. When that didn't work, he figured out the play at the cabin, where McAllister and I were bound to tangle, but he didn't count on McAllister getting bumped or Gale making an appearance.

"Were you seeing her?" she asked pointedly.

"Gale?"

"Yes."

"I kept her close because I suspicioned she was wrapped up in the answer to the riddle one way or another. She started the ball rolling by coming to my office, so I figured she had to know more than what she was letting on." I hoped my answer would suffice, but somehow I knew Teri realized Gale had meant more to me than I cared to admit. Teri could always see through me.

"It seems so unreal. I still can't believe it."

"Yeah, me, too," I agreed. I took one of her hands in mine and looked into her eyes. "So where does this leave us, Teri?" I asked softly.

She squeezed my hand and tears welled up in her eyes. "I'm so sorry, Nick. Part of me wants to be with you more than anything in the world, but a bigger part of me knows it will never work. We'll always have what happened hanging over our heads in the background. You're strong, but I can't live with seeing you every day and the constant reminder of everything that's happened," she said as tears streamed down her cheeks.

My chest tightened up and my breathing became painful. "What are you saying, Teri?" I asked heavily.

"I'm going out West to start over and try to forget. A friend of mine has offered to share her place in Boise. What about you? What will you do now?"

"I don't know. I've always loved you. This time I thought it was for keeps."

She sobbed aloud while I concentrated on my breathing, trying to gain control of my own feelings. When her crying slowed, she stood up, leaned over, kissed me on the cheek, and whispered, "Take care of yourself, Nick," and walked out. It was the second time I lost her.

Chapter Forty-one

Two weeks later

When the car pulled up to the curb, the driver got out and loaded my bags into the trunk. I asked him to drive north and turnaround for one last drive down Lake Shore Drive. We slowly made our way along Michigan Avenue, past my office, the sun was setting, casting a blood-orange hue across the lazy waves on the lake. I gave a small nod of homage when I looked up at my office window and the life I was leaving behind.

I had paid up my office and apartment leases, and left a forwarding address in the unlikely event either place was subleased and I had a refund coming. I signed my car title over to Louie and told him to keep whatever he received from selling my rust bucket.

Two days later, I reached the coast by rail. A porter unloaded my bags, and attached identification tags to each piece of luggage before he ripped off the receipts and handed them to me. I tipped him a buck and went into the terminal. A glance at one of the schedule boards revealed the embarkation information.

After clearing customs, I took my time walking to the passenger loading area. As I approached the gangplank, a familiar face appeared out of the waiting crowd. "All set, Nick?"

"As much as I'll ever be," I answered.

"You don't seem to be here, man. You okay, Nick?"

"Sorry, Bobby, I was just thinking about what a fellow by the name of Montaigne once said, "A man is not hurt so much by what happens, as by his opinion of what happens."

"You've lost me. What're you saying, Nick?"

"I'll never take life so serious again. It's time to live it up to the fullest. C'mon, let's board and I'll buy you a drink as soon as we're out to sea." Taking him by the arm, I led him up the gangplank, my step lighter.

John Gay had it right: 'Life is a jest, and all things show it. I thought it once, and now I know it.'

"Bobby, did I ever tell you about the gal I met in Paris during the war?"

"Does she have a sister?"

Nicolas D. Charles secludes himself in the north woods of Wisconsin. This is the first book in the *Nick Verriet: The Early Years* series. Visit his website at www.nickverriet.com.